# DARLING MINX

The Benningtons
Book 4

## ANNABELLE MARIN

Published by Blushing Books
An Imprint of
ABCD Graphics and Design, Inc.
A Virginia Corporation
977 Seminole Trail #233
Charlottesville, VA 22901

Darling Minx
Annabelle Marin

EBook ISBN: 978-1-63954-561-2
Print ISBN: 978-1-63954-562-9

# The Bennington Family Tree

Paul Bennington (1821-1870)
Petunia Bennington (1822-1859)
Christopher Bennington (b.1840. 30 years old)
Steve Bennington (b.1842. 28 years old)
Hugh Bennington (b.1845. 25 years old)
Poppy Bennington (b.1845. 25 years old)
Anthony Bennington (b.1849. 21 years old)
Iris Bennington (b.1855. 15 years old)
Lily Bennington (b.1859. 11 years old)

# Chapter 1

LARKSPUR VALLEY, *Wyoming, January 1873*

"Please don't go."

Twenty-eight-year-old Dr. Hugh Bennington sighed, running his palm down his face in frustration as he looked at his fraternal twin sister Poppy Bennington. She had become Mrs. Weston last year, after being a spinster for longer than she should have been.

She was looking at him as if he had just announced he was going to war, which was an exaggeration on her part. He was just going to Laramie, the nearest city, which was less than a day's journey by train. It was also the same city where Hugh and his younger brother Anthony had attended school.

Unfortunately, all of the trains were currently out of commission because of all the snow Larkspur Valley had received. As a result, Hugh was forced to make the journey by horse, which took considerably longer. Fortunately, he was a fast rider.

While he and Poppy shared the same blue eyes all of the Bennington siblings had, their hair color was different. Hugh had the same inky black hair as his brothers while Poppy's own hair was a buttery yellow.

Her husband, Finn Weston, wrapped an arm protectively around his wife while giving Hugh a reproachful look. Poppy was four months pregnant, the little belly ballooning underneath her thick wool dress. Since the announcement of her pregnancy, her husband had waited on her hand and foot, as if Finn couldn't be more pathetic.

Finn and Hugh had never really seen eye to eye. as he was more the older brothers Christopher and Steve's friend rather than Hugh's. Hugh thought Finn was a lovesick fool who lacked a spine because he'd been pining after Poppy for years. Finn, on the other hand, considered Hugh rude and selfish, which Hugh had to admit wasn't exactly a lie.

"I'll be back before you know it, Pop." Hugh patted her head affectionately. His sisters, especially his twin, were the only ones who managed to bring out his softer side. "I'll only be gone for a few days."

Hugh's favorite cigars had been unavailable for months. Mr. Simon, the owner of the mercantile, had assured him he simply hadn't received his packages, but Hugh had a feeling it was because the Benningtons had been less than kind to his beast of a daughter, Chrissy.

As a result, he had to make the journey into the city, which was the reason for his sister's fussy nature. Hugh had to go now, as it was the first time in months he hadn't had to deliver a baby, no one was sick and no one was dying. If he didn't go now, he wouldn't have a decent break until the summer, after he delivered Poppy's baby.

She wrinkled her nose. "I still don't understand why you are going all the way over there for cigars. It's such a nasty habit, Hugh. Mr. Howard from church is convinced cigars will end up killing men someday."

"Mr. Howard also believes that one day, we will be able

to roam the skies like birds. I wouldn't take his words to heart, sis."

Poppy looked like she was going to argue, but Finn interrupted, "Let him go, sweetheart, he's a grown man. He knows what he's doing. Don't guilt yourself. Whatever foolish decision he makes is his alone."

Hugh scowled at him.

Poppy bit her lower lip worriedly. "Just hurry home, Hugh. The weather is so terrible, I worry about you. The last thing I need is for you to be lost in a snowstorm."

His sister thought that just because he didn't have a wife fussing over him, Hugh must surely be incompetent. Being blissfully in love and being their wives' lapdogs might suit Christopher and Steve fine, but Hugh enjoyed having the company of a different woman every night.

He had never been one to form strong, loving relationships outside his family, never properly courted a woman. Hugh thought most women were boring and had the attention span of a bird. Hugh would probably remain a bachelor forever, which suited him just fine. His work as a doctor kept him perfectly busy.

"I'll be back in two shakes of a lamb's tail, Pop." Hugh kissed her forehead. "Just focus on keeping my little niece or nephew safe in your belly."

Hugh didn't bother saying goodbye to Finn. The air was bitterly cold as he got on top of his horse and headed towards Laramie. Hugh hadn't bothered telling the rest of his siblings about his little trip; he would let Poppy squeal like she always did.

Besides, Hugh doubted any of his siblings besides Poppy would notice he was gone. Christopher and Steve were busy with their families, Anthony was busy as the church pastor, Iris spent every minute of the day studying so she could pass her teaching exam, and Lily was no doubt busy scrapbooking or doing whatever young girls currently obsessed over.

Not to mention, Hugh was in no mood to hear a scolding delivered by his older brothers. He loved them, but Chris and Steve still treated him like a troubled fourteen-year-old at times. No, it was better this way. The less they knew, the better. Hugh would just pick up six months' worth of cigars and return back to Larkspur Valley.

Once or twice, he thought about hiring another doctor to help him at his practice, but then he was quickly reminded that he was annoyed by most people, leading him to dismiss the idea. It was better this way. Hugh was, and would always be, a loner.

The trip to Laramie turned out to be more of a hassle than he had anticipated. For starters, the trip by horse went mind-numbingly slow compared to traveling by train. Even though Hugh was an expert rider growing up on a successful cattle ranch, he didn't particularly enjoy riding in the blistering cold.

Hugh longed for a Wyoming summer. At least then, he didn't have to deal with the sudden occurrence of snowstorms or an endless amount of patients who only came in for a sniffle.

When he finally made it to the city and secured his packages, Hugh briefly wondered how his life would have been different if he had moved to the city to open his practice instead of returning to his childhood home of Larkspur Valley.

He would probably be earning more money, there would be more entertaining things for him to do, and he would no doubt be surrounded by lovelier women than he had in his dull little town.

Anthony, his pestering little brother, had asked him once why he didn't just stay in the city, but Hugh had ignored him.

The reality was he would have missed his family too much. Even though Laramie wasn't far from Larkspur Valley, Hugh would have still felt the emptiness. The years he had spent away attending medical school had been hard enough. Besides, his family might be a pain at times, but they stuck up for each other, and his parents' graves were in Larkspur Valley. He couldn't leave.

Hugh stayed the night at an inn in the city and even kept his promise to his twin and was good, by not hiring a prostitute. The next morning, he ventured back to Larkspur Valley, silently cursing himself for being so stupid and coming into the city in the midst of this unpredictable weather.

Hugh wasn't much of a worrier, but even he was concerned as snow started coming down. His horse started whining in protest. He had lived through enough Wyoming winters to know this was a snowstorm that was preparing to descend on him.

The middle Bennington brother continued on his path even though he wasn't quite sure where he was going. There wasn't anything out here for miles. Continuing was better than staying where he was and freezing to death. The last thing he needed was for his siblings to find his corpse.

He breathed a sigh of relief and thanked the God he wasn't even sure existed when he found a small cabin. It was shabby and not well made, but it was better than nothing. Best of all, it looked abandoned, so he didn't have to beg for shelter or make small talk.

Hugh opened the door and frowned. He had been expecting it to be empty, but it actually looked cozy.

Someone did live here if the shabby couches, cracked plates and cups, and clean laundry all over the place were any indication.

He cleared his throat, touching his pistol inside his coat pocket. His brother Steve, the sheriff of Larkspur Valley, always told him to carry a weapon in case of emergencies. Chris and he followed the rule dutifully, while Anthony thought they were silly. But then again, he was a pastor.

Hugh wasn't a fan of shooting anyone, mainly because it was a pain to pull the bullet out of someone. Still, he wasn't opposed to defending himself. To be honest, he liked a little violence, which was why he had almost been kicked out of medical school for all of the fights he had gotten himself in.

"Hello? Is anyone here?" He cleared his throat as he put on a cheerful, fake voice. "I am not here to hurt anyone. I would just like a place to stay for the night. My name is Dr. Hugh Bennington."

Silence.

Hugh smiled. Maybe the place was abandoned after all. Lucky him.

He started looking around the small kitchen, desperate for food, but he found only tea bags and a small loaf of stale bread. Hugh scoffed as he closed the cabinet. Thankfully, he had brought a bit of food with him; he was hopeful it would last him until the storm died off.

A pair of lacy drawers caught his attention as he picked them up. They were small and delicate looking, which made him wonder why women liked lacy, unpractical underthings if they were just going to be ripped by their husbands.

The door flew open as Hugh turned around, still holding on to the lacy underthings. He was ready to pull out his gun if necessary.

A woman stood before him, dressed messily in men's winter clothes which were too big on her small frame. She was carrying a pathetic amount of wood and her bright red curls were stuck to her forehead.

The woman's eyes widened when she saw him holding on to her lacy drawers. "Don't touch that!"

Her face flushed adorably, obviously not expecting him

inside her property. Hugh was glad she didn't have a husband; otherwise, he would have probably beaten Hugh to a bloody pulp.

She took a step forward, no doubt ready to smack him. Her eyes widened when she felt her foot slip as she tumbled backwards, feet up in the air.

Hugh heard her head hit the wet floor before she became still. He groaned. He really did have the worst luck in the world. Now, he had to play savior.

## Chapter 2

SUSANNAH CASSIDY'S teeth chattered as she tied the small, frail pieces of wood with a piece of an old sheet she had torn up just this morning. The amount of wood she had in front of her was pathetic, but she had to rely on whatever branches the nearby trees had tossed. She couldn't wield the heavy ax, and wasting money paying for lumber was a fool's choice. Not that she had the money to pay for it, either, not to mention the horse and wagon had been one of the first things sold in order to give her dear late husband, Harry, a decent funeral.

Susannah let out a series of curses as her frail fingers struggled to tie the sheet holding the wood. Her hands were trembling as if they belonged to an eighty-year-old woman and not a twenty-five-year-old.

When she finally managed to tie her package, she breathed a sigh of relief. Susannah managed to place the package over her shoulder as she made her way back to her little farm. Susannah had three coats over her dress, her husband's old boots, Harry's old hat, a scarf, and gloves, yet she was still freezing.

Susannah had lived in Wyoming for seven years, since she and Harry had married and come in their little wagon from Kansas. She sighed. That seemed so long ago, when they had been young and full of dreams.

A chill knocked down her hat, but she was too cold and too tired to get it. Harry would surely understand. Besides, he hated that hat; he used to say it made his ears look too big. She smiled at the memory.

This had to be the worst winter in Wyoming history, she thought as she trudged along.

Susannah's entire body trembled from the cold. She was surprised she was still able to move at all. It felt like her lips and limbs were frozen. Her eyelids felt heavy, almost like her body longed to go to sleep, but she refused to allow it. Falling asleep outside in the snow, was a guaranteed death. Many people had died that way and Susannah wouldn't be another victim.

She just had to get home, build her meager little fire, and settle down with a nice cup of tea while she tried to ignore her rumbling belly. There was very little food left in the cupboard and she had to make it stretch until the elderly Mr. Wilson could take her into the city once the snow stopped falling.

After her husband's death two years ago, she had relied on the neighbors' pity, but pity only went on for so long. They all urged her to return to Kansas, but she didn't have any money and her only family, Ma and Pa, had died of tuberculosis shortly after she and Harry settled in Wyoming.

And she couldn't leave the farm. It was Harry's dream, and now that he was gone, she supposed it ought to be her dream too.

They had left Kansas in search of better opportunities, and as Harry had mentioned, better growing soil. Harry had planned on growing corn, sugar beets, and lettuce, but when the first two years brought dismal growth, he'd tried his hand at hog raising and butchering. The next two years were hard, and Susannah shuddered when she remembered how sticky her hands had felt with pig grease and how disgusting butchering time was. But she had done it all to help Harry.

The last year Harry had been alive had been the worst one yet. The little money they had earned from hog raising had been used to pay Harry's medical bills when he'd become sick. The doctor hadn't been quite sure what illness Harry had. Only that his illness had been "in the bones" because Harry's joints had become painful the last few months before his death and he had struggled to move them.

Before dying, Harry had made Susannah promise she would keep working on the farm.

It had been a loud, tiring, depressing journey. For the past two years since Harry's death, Susannah had been trying her best to keep her promise to her late husband. She had tried her hand at corn growing again, since hogs were too much work for just one person, but her crop, so far, had been pitiful.

Susannah had been relying on the few vegetables she'd managed to grow and the money she had received from selling her and Harry's personal belongings. It had been painful, but she hadn't had anything else she could sell.

Tears pooled in her eyes when she wondered what would become of her. She had no money and nothing else of value. With her luck, she would end up as a lady of the night.

She breathed a sigh of relief when she approached her warm little cabin. Her stomach grumbled angrily. "Not to worry, I am almost there," she mumbled. "Then we will have a cup of hot tea."

Susannah struggled to twist the doorknob with her trem-bling hands, but she finally did. She expected to find her sitting room exactly as she had left it, pitiful and pathetic, but neat.

Instead, her green eyes flew open at the scene in front of her. There was a man in her tiny kitchen. A tall, strong man by the looks of it, or maybe it was his thick winter riding coat which made him look bulky.

The man had thick, glossy black hair the color of coal, perfectly preserved despite the harsh winds. His skin was a rosy-pink due to the cold and his eyes were a harsh blue which gave him an unfriendly demeanor.

There was a pinched look on his face, as if her poverty was beneath him. Who was this man? What was he doing here? Was he a murderer? Worse, a debt collector?

Susannah opened her mouth to speak, but nothing came out, while her legs shook like the cranberry jelly Mama had made during her last Thanksgiving at home.

She finally made a squealing sound like a piglet when she saw that he held her lacy drawers in his hands. "Don't touch that!"

A man hadn't been inside her home touching her things since Harry died. It felt unwelcome and unnatural.

Susannah moved her foot forward, but it was still slippery due to the snow and she ended up tumbling backwards, feet up in the air.

She felt a sharp pain in the back of her head before everything went black.

---

*Seven years ago*

"It's not much," Harry said sheepishly as the young, eighteen-year-old couple made their way inside the small cabin he had built for them.

Susannah peeked inside, an excited smile on her face.

After riding in a covered wagon for months and sleeping inside it or on the ground during their travels, she was just excited to sleep somewhere with an actual roof.

She pushed back her sunbonnet until it was hanging loosely around her neck. Her green eyes shone excitedly as she looked at the small cabin that her darling husband had built with his own two hands. It reminded her of the home she had lived in with Ma and Pa, back in Kansas. Harry had even started building furniture.

The young woman touched her flat stomach. She hoped Harry knew how to build a crib when the time came. She couldn't wait to be a mother and she thought the small farm in Wyoming would be the perfect place to raise a family.

"I promise I will make it grander," Harry quickly promised, taking her silence as disappointment. "You'll see, Sue, as soon as the first crops come next year, we'll have enough money to make the house bigger and buy you as many Sunday dresses as you want."

"The church is so far away, Harry." Susannah giggled as she wrapped her arms around her husband. "I love our little place because it was made with your own two hands. Thank you, Harry."

Harry looked at her in adoration. "You sure you won't regret coming to Wyoming and being a farmer's wife, my darling Sue?"

Susannah shook her head. "Never. Our farm will be successful; you'll see. Our children will take it over when we are old and gray. We'll tell them how Grandpa Harry and Grandma Susannah came to Wyoming to follow their dreams."

## Chapter 3

SUSANNAH JANE CASSIDY.

The only reason Hugh knew the fainting woman's name was because she had stupidly sewn her name on every piece of clothing she owned, even her drawers. Not even Lily, his baby sister who was still a child, did that.

Hugh hoped Susannah would wake up, then they would be able to brush away this incredibly embarrassing moment, and he would be on his merry way. Hugh would sleep in a tree as long as he didn't have to be near this dramatic woman.

Hugh had no patience for hysterical women, especially when his sisters—excluding Lily—and his sisters-in-law—with the exception of Ruby—were all practical women.

However, she did not wake up and, instead, seemed to grow paler, to the point he could see the slight veins poking from under her pale skin.

He started shaking her slightly, hoping she would wake up. Susannah didn't move.

"Susannah," he growled. "Wake up! Susannah! Now is not the time to sleep."

Susannah didn't budge. This was when he noticed her wet clothes were sticking to her body and her cheeks were flushed, while the rest of her face was pale. He pressed a hand against her forehead. Definitely a fever.

Could be the beginning signs of influenza or pneumonia.

Hugh groaned. He couldn't just leave her alone now. His conscience wouldn't let him, especially since the woman didn't seem to have a husband, even with the ring on her finger, nor children.

He scooped her up, surprised at how light she was despite the wet clothes she was wearing. He didn't think she weighed much more than Lily.

There was a small bed in the tiny bedroom at the back of the house. He was surprised how comfortable someone could be in such a small cabin. Then again, his own father had made sure each of his seven children had their own bedroom growing up, so he wasn't used to being cramped. Even his bachelor home had three perfectly sized bedrooms.

Susannah stirred a bit in her sleep as soon as he put her down on the bed. Then her eyes flew open. Green eyes, the color of pine trees, stared back at him. Her mouth opened slightly, giving her the appearance of a frightened rabbit.

Hugh gripped her by the shoulders as gently as he could so she didn't stand up in a panic, especially since he didn't know how hard she had hit her head.

"Mrs. Cassidy," he said calmly, in a way that was supposed to make her more comfortable, but which only seemed to make her panic more. "My name is Dr. Hugh Bennington. I'm sorry for intruding. Please don't move. You might have injured your head. I was caught in the snow and thought this cabin was abandoned."

Susannah shook her head as she struggled to speak. "My husband, Harry, and I live here."

"Where is Harry?"

What kind of man left his wife alone to gather wood in the middle of a snowstorm? His married brothers would first cut off their limbs before exposing their wives to such dangers.

"D-dead."

Then she fainted.

Hugh sighed as he looked at her. It seemed he could never truly escape his work. Thankfully, he was good at what he did.

What he needed to do next, was get Susannah out of these wet clothes. Thankfully, she was passed out and he didn't have to deal with her silly female sensibilities. His sister-in-law, Ruby, accused him of having a poor bedside manner, but Hugh didn't understand what was so embarrassing about the human body.

Hugh had seen plenty of humans naked. Women should consider themselves lucky that they had a more attractive figure than males.

His large, rough hands removed her wet clothes from her body. They were thin, completely ruined by the snow. Then he removed her chemise, corset, and drawers, until Susannah was fully naked.

Hugh managed to find a nightgown draped over one of the ugly looking chairs in her bedroom and kept it handy. She didn't seem to have a cough, so it couldn't be pneumonia; not that influenza was much better.

When he looked at her nude body, he frowned. It didn't take a genius to see that she was malnourished. He could see her ribs and hip bones under the layer of pale skin. Bruises, some old and some new, trailed down her body in yellow, purple, and black. Her hands were red and dry. While Hugh guessed that, as a redhead, she bruised easily, there was quite the possibility Susannah had been doing the farm work by herself.

Working in the fields was hard work, especially for a woman. His father had never allowed his sisters nor his mother to work on the ranch. Christopher had even refused to let his wife, Lucy, assist him in any way, with the exception of feeding the chickens.

Women belonged at home. Men belonged making the money while making their wives' lives more pleasant. He wondered briefly if Susannah had married a useless idiot. From their brief encounter, he could tell she wasn't the brightest, either.

Susannah shivered, almost as if she could sense Hugh was thinking rude thoughts. He quickly made a fire with the sticks she had brought. It wasn't much. He would have to chop down some more wood when the snowstorm had passed. Surely, there was an ax somewhere.

Afterwards, he made his way back to the deserted barn to place his horse in for the night. Hugh grabbed his medical bag he always carried with him before he returned to Susannah's room.

Susannah had curled up into a tight little ball in his absence and he could see the small, round cheeks of her ass along with the sweet petals of her sex.

Hugh, ever the professional, ignored the beautiful woman in favor of making her more comfortable. He placed some awful smelling balm on her bruises, which made her skin sticky and caused Susannah to wrinkle her nose in her sleep.

He pulled out a thick thermometer from his black bag, then some salve which would make the insertion easier.

His hands parted her cheeks, exposing her tight, pink rosebud. Hugh coated his pinky with the salve instead of his index finger, to make the insertion easier, before he started inserting it gently into her rectum.

He used his pinky finger to stretch her, but she was unbearably tight.

Susannah squirmed and whined in her sleep but didn't wake up, indicating her fever must be high if she was able to sleep through it.

After he'd decided she was stretched enough, he inserted the thermometer, keeping both hands pressed against her small cheeks to keep her from pushing it out of her rectum in her sleep.

When a few minutes passed, he pulled it out while Susannah pressed her face against the pillow like a sleepy kitten.

Hugh read the thermometer—one hundred and two degrees. No wonder she had fainted, with a fever this high, no doubt aggravating it more by going outside in the bitter cold.

He would scold her later. The doctor placed the nightgown on her, then covered her with every blanket he could find. His fingers touched the back of her head searching for a bump from her earlier fall, but he didn't find any.

Given his medical education, Hugh probably shouldn't let her sleep, in case she had a concussion, but she looked exhausted and he needed her fever to drop. A few hours of sleep wouldn't kill her.

The lack of any other available beds left a dilemma for Hugh as he settled on a nearby chair since the couch in the sitting room looked uncomfortable. He didn't want to be far away from Susannah, in case she woke in the middle of the night and startled herself when she saw him.

Hugh was drifting off to sleep when he heard Susannah mumble something along the lines of, "Oh, Harry."

"No, it's Hugh," he mumbled sleepily before he also fell asleep.

Susannah felt as if she were a cake being baked in the oven. Nice and warm.

Warm. That had been something she hadn't been feeling for the past few months. Perhaps she had died and gone to Heaven to be with Harry?

Susannah jolted herself awake at the thought. No, she couldn't die. At least not yet. She had promised her husband she would take care of the farm.

Susannah's green eyes opened as she sat up. She regretted the motion a second later when a wave of dizziness hit her from sitting up so fast. She was in her bedroom. How had she made it here? The last thing she remembered was struggling to open the door and get away from the blistering cold.

She bit her lower lip. There had been a man. A man who had been holding her drawers. Was it possible he was still there? Or had it all been a dream? Oh, how she wished Harry was there. Living alone in the country was unheard of for a woman, and she guessed she was lucky she wasn't dead yet.

Susannah slowly got up, even though every part of her body ached and it felt like she was walking underwater. Shivers exploded through her body as she wondered if she was feverish.

She slowly made her way to her bedroom door, her clammy hands gripping an umbrella that was perched against the armoire.

Oh, how she wished she had a gun, but Harry had thought guns were unsafe. Not that she would be able to shoot one anyway.

Susannah slowly opened the door just a bit. Her whole body started trembling when she saw the back of the large man from earlier, recognizing him by his inky black hair. He seemed to be reading while sitting on her chair.

Gripping the umbrella in her hand, she lunged towards him. It was now or never.

The man let out a series of curse words when the umbrella landed on his head. He turned furiously towards Susannah. His eyes were an ice blue and he looked absolutely furious, almost like a mad man.

Susannah stopped in her tracks. He was going to kill her; she could just taste it.

"What is wrong with you, you lunatic? You could have seriously hurt someone." He took the umbrella from her and tossed it across the room. "I should smack your bottom so you can feel the same pain I'm feeling, Susannah."

"W-what?" Her voice was shaking. Oh, no, it always shook when she was about to cry. She did not want to cry in front of this man.

The man frowned. "You don't remember me? What are you doing out of bed? You're still sick."

"I remember you barging into my house unannounced." She didn't mention the drawer part. It was too embarrassing. "Who are you? How do you know my name?"

"I didn't know this was your house. I was just trying to find shelter from the snow." He scoffed. "And I know your name because you've sewn your initials or your full name, Susannah Jane Cassidy, on every pillowcase, hankie, and piece of clothing, like a toddler."

Susannah blushed, but she refused to acknowledge his insults. Where were this man's manners? "It stopped snowing," she replied coldly. "And I suggest you continue on your way home Mr.—"

"Dr. Hugh Bennington, and I'm not going anywhere." He scooped her up in his strong arms, catching her by surprise. "At least not until you are well."

She blinked as he deposited her on the bed. "Well?"

"You have a mild case of influenza; you've been sleeping it off for the past two days." He touched her cheek. "You're lucky I came along, or it could have been much worse. Thankfully, you didn't have a cough. It seemed what you needed was a warm bed to sleep in."

Now, Susannah felt ungrateful. "Thank you for your help, Dr. Bennington—"

"Please call me Hugh."

"Hugh. I'm afraid I have no money to pay for your services."

"You have given me room and board, which is plenty." He looked around. "Now, where is your husband? I believe you mentioned his name was Harry."

"Yes, it is," she replied softly as she reached for her finger to touch her wedding ring. She had thought about pawning it to pay off bills and purchase food years ago but found she couldn't do it. She would have never forgiven herself. "He passed away two years ago. I'm a widow."

"I'm sorry to hear that. You mentioned it before you became unconscious, but I wanted to verify." Hugh's voice sounded robotic and he didn't sound too sorry at all, but she was beginning to think it was just his personality.

"He had an illness; the doctors in the city could never figure out what it was," she blurted.

Hugh nodded. "Wait here. Get under the covers."

Susannah did as she was told. She had a feeling people seldom refused Hugh's orders. It was quite obvious the man had a temper, but even if he was less than nice, he had still saved her. She supposed she ought to be polite to him.

The doctor reentered the room a few minutes later, carrying a tray with a bowl of steaming broth and a cup of hot tea. "It's not much, I'm afraid, but you didn't have food in your kitchen. I had to use what I brought for myself."

Susannah wondered in amazement at how someone could be thoughtful and rude all at once. She stared at the bowl of broth. The food did look appetizing. The tea was less so, as it was an awful green color.

Her stomach growled painfully and she blushed. Picking up the spoon, she brought some food to her lips. "It's good," she replied in surprise. "You can cook."

Hugh shrugged. "Just the basics. As a bachelor, you have to learn to survive."

It was the first time Susannah noticed he didn't have a wedding ring. She wondered if he had a sweetheart back home. She doubted many women could stand him.

"Stop staring at me and eat," he interrupted her thoughts harshly. "Don't just stare. Don't eat too fast, or it will come back again. Your stomach has been empty for two days. Drink your tea too. I made it with my special herb recipe. It shall take care of the last bit of fever you have."

Susannah finished the broth first, which was delicious, before she moved on to the tea. She wrinkled her nose adorably when she was hit with the stench. It smelled odd, like rotten fish and spoiled milk.

How bad could it be? The broth had been good.

She took a sip and immediately looked for somewhere to spit out the liquid. She didn't care how rude it was.

Hugh must have sensed this because he pressed a hand against her jaw to keep it closed. "Swallow."

Her eyes watered even though he was holding her jaw gently. She swallowed the bitter liquid before she stuck out her tongue. "It's disgusting."

"Perhaps, but it works," he replied calmly as he pushed the cup towards her. "I didn't bring any medicine and the weather is too unpredictable for me to head into the city. You're lucky your influenza didn't turn into pneumonia, but you are still not well. You have a fever. Not to mention, you're severely malnourished. Drink the tea, Susannah. It is the only way you will get better." His eyes flashed darkly. "Don't make me force you, because I will. It won't be pretty if I do."

She flushed, doing as she was told even though her eyes watered and her stomach recoiled with every sip. "I can't do it anymore," she whimpered, her eyes filled with tears. "Please don't make me."

Perhaps in a rare moment of sympathy, he took the cup away from her. "Fine, but you're having the rest tomorrow after breakfast."

A sigh of relief escaped her lips. "What time is it?"

"Around six in the evening. You've been sleeping for the past day and a half or so, which is just what you needed. You're making a quick recovery, which is unusual in patients."

Her chest fluttered at his rare praise.

"Where are you from, Hugh? Are you from Laramie?"

"No, but I went to school there." Hugh placed his hand inside his medical bag and pulled out a rather large thermometer and a jar of salve. "I live in a small town out east called Larkspur Valley. It's only a couple of days' journey by horse, but it's more convenient to ride by train these days."

She'd never ridden on a train before. She and Harry could have never afforded it. Susannah wanted to ask what it was like, but she was too embarrassed to ask him. "Why did you ride all the way to Laramie in the middle of a snowstorm?"

He shrugged. "Cigars."

Susannah blinked in disbelief. "Excuse me? You rode all this way for cigars?"

"They are my favorite." He shrugged. "Besides, I have no wife, no kids, and no patients at home. With everyone stuck at home because of the snowstorm, it was the perfect time to go." He slapped the mattress. "Get on your belly."

"Why?"

"I need to take your temperature."

Susannah blushed bright red. "You're putting the ther-mometer in—"

"In your rectum, yes," he continued for her when she was too embarrassed to say the word. "I need to make sure you don't have a fever."

Susannah hadn't gotten her temperature taken since she was a little girl, but she remembered how uncomfortable it had been.

"I'm fine. All better, see." She gave Hugh a nervous smile, but he didn't look the least bit amused. "There really is no need. My fever is all gone."

"Then let me check." Hugh's face had lost all trace of amusement and it was replaced by irritation. "Influenza can take a nasty turn even when you think you're on the road to recovery." He pulled back the covers as Susannah pressed a pillow to her chest.

"Susannah," he growled. "Don't make me cross. I am quite willing to tie your ankles and arms to the bedframe if that's the only way I can examine you."

Her eyes widened before she slowly turned on her belly. Hugh seemed like the type of man who would make good on his threat.

The doctor seemed satisfied. "Good girl."

When she was lying fully on her stomach, Hugh pulled up her nightgown. She buried her burning face in one of the pillow as she imagined Hugh looking at her small, round buttocks. No one had ever seen her naked, with the excep-tion of Harry.

Not to mention, she was too skinny and hadn't had a proper bath since she'd fainted. Her nervous thoughts were interrupted when she felt Hugh part her cheeks. His large index finger started covering her tight rosebud with the salve.

Susannah squeaked as she attempted to move. Hugh caught her quickly and slapped the back of one thigh. "Stop moving, Susannah. Honestly, you act like a child."

She didn't like being scolded like a child, but she was too embarrassed to say anything.

When the thermometer went in, she tried her best to remain still even though it was uncomfortable. Hugh must have noticed her efforts because he started rubbing her lower back. "Good girl. We're almost done."

*Good girl.* She liked hearing those words come out of his lips. Harry had never called her a good girl.

Susannah shook her head. What on earth was she thinking? Harry had been her lawfully wedded husband. Dr. Bennington was just a stranger who was offering to help her out. She should be ashamed at her impure thoughts.

"Why is your body covered in bruises? Is anyone being cruel to you?"

"No." She was surprised by his question and how fiercely protective he was being. "My skin is very fair. Being a redhead, it bruises easily." She cleared her throat. "Farm work is hard work. When Harry was here, he would do the heavy lifting, but when he died, it was up to me to continue working on the farm. I'm not very strong nor tall. Half the time, I struggle to carry a pile of wood, as you have been privy to. The bruises are just an example of that. No one has hurt me, only my lack of physical strength."

"Taking care of a farm is hard work for a woman as frail as you. Have you always lived in Wyoming?"

"No. Harry and I originally came from Kansas in search of a better life. Harry thought it would be easy to have a successful farm in only a year or two. He read in the newspaper how Wyoming soil is fertile and perfect for farming. Luck, I'm afraid, wasn't on our side."

"Farming is harder than most people anticipate. Crops are harder to tame than animals. Why didn't you return to Kansas after Harry died?"

"I didn't have any money. Paying for a funeral is expensive." Susannah couldn't believe how honest she was being with this complete stranger, but Hugh was easy to talk to. "Besides, shortly after I married Harry, my parents died."

"No siblings?"

"None."

"Aunts? Uncles? Cousins?"

"None. My family was very small. Not many relatives. Now that Harry is gone, it's just me."

He removed the thermometer from her butt and she quickly placed her nightgown down to preserve what little modesty she had left.

"What about you? Do you have any siblings?"

"Six." He grinned.

Susannah's eyes widened. She couldn't imagine having such a large family. "Are they all doctors, like you?"

"No, but they all live in Larkspur Valley."

"Are you the oldest?"

"No, that would be Christopher. Since he's the oldest, he runs the family's cattle ranch with his wife, Lucy. They have a baby boy named Lloyd. After him, is my brother Steve, who is the town sheriff. He's married to Ruby and they have a little girl, Silver. My twin sister and I are next in line."

Susannah looked curious. "What is your sister's name?"

"Poppy, but we call her Pop. She married last year." His mouth curled and she wondered if he was unhappy with the marriage. "She and my brother-in-law, Finn, are expecting a baby which shall be born in the late spring."

Susannah clapped her hands in glee. She loved babies,

and she thought it would be wonderful to be surrounded by so many nieces, nephews, and in-laws. She'd never experience it. Even Harry had come from a small family. "You must be a proud uncle."

Hugh nodded, smiling for the first time. "They are a lovable bunch."

"What about the rest of your siblings? Are they married as well?"

He shook his head. "Anthony is a pastor and is so busy preaching, he pays no attention to courting. Iris is graduating from school in May, but she's let us know she won't marry and, instead, is content to teach school." Hugh wrinkled his nose. He obviously didn't agree with a woman working, even though Susannah thought it was modern. "My youngest sister, Lily, is still only a baby. We don't have to worry about her for a few more years."

"How old is she?"

"She'll be turning fourteen this year."

Susannah laughed. "Oh, Hugh, that's not a baby."

"Well, she's the youngest, so it makes her the baby," he said defensively. "Enough about me, you need to go back to bed."

Susannah had been too busy hearing about Hugh's family, she didn't notice her full bladder until now. "Um, Hugh, I need to use the outhouse."

Hugh frowned. "It's starting to snow again. I don't want you to go outside. You might get sick again and your fever just started going down."

The pressure in her bladder became harder to ignore. "Well, I really need to go."

"Harry should have built an outhouse which connected to the house. That's what my brothers and I did."

"Well, we didn't. I only need a minute."

Hugh's frown deepened while her desperation grew. She was going to urinate on herself if he didn't hurry.

"Hugh!"

"Give me a minute." He disappeared into the kitchen and came back with a couple of rags and a small bucket that she had used to feed the chickens when they first had them. "Here, you can use this."

"I can't! It's a bucket."

Even when they had been traveling, there had been a small bush where she could have a bit of privacy.

"Susannah," he warned, "don't test me. I am not letting you go outside."

"Fine!" Susannah stood up in a mix of anger and embarrassment. She must have stood up too fast, because a wave of dizziness hit her. Hugh managed to wrap an arm around her waist before she fell.

"Are you all right?" he asked gruffly. "Don't get up so fast. You were in bed for a few days. Your body needs to get used to standing up."

She ignored his concerns. All she could think about was how she was expected to pee in a bucket in front of this handsome man.

"Go outside," Susannah ordered. "I will not have you here while I am doing my business."

Hugh hesitated, but finally allowed her to have some privacy. When he had departed to the sitting room, she quickly lifted up her nightgown, squatted, and emptied her bladder. Afterwards, she emptied the bucket by opening the window of her bedroom, not caring if it earned her another scolding.

Thankfully, there was a pitcher of water and some soap on her vanity table which she quickly used to wash her hands and give the bucket a quick rinse. She couldn't remember the last time she'd been so embarrassed.

"Get back into bed," Hugh ordered when she finally let him back in.

"Where do you sleep?" She yawned, doing as she was told.

"In the sitting room."

"Those chairs are uncomfortable," she mumbled, already half asleep.

Hugh grabbed the chair from her vanity table to sit in front of her while she lay in bed. His voice was soft, masculine. "I manage, Susannah."

## Chapter 4

SUNLIGHT STREAMED through the only window in the bedroom, hitting Hugh right in the face. He scowled then rubbed his face. He hated waking up so early in the morning and if he didn't have his own medical practice or a brother who was a pastor who dragged him into church every Sunday without fail, he would probably sleep until noon.

He sat up in confusion when he noticed Susannah wasn't beside him. Both of them must have fallen asleep after they had talked long into the night—well, Susannah had babbled while he politely listened. The widow was sick, after all, and her life was already terrible enough without him being rude.

Hugh had planned on sleeping on Susannah's hard couch when she had fallen asleep; it was the gentlemanly thing to do after all, but he must have fallen asleep from exhaustion. Thankfully, Susannah hadn't panicked like other females. The problem was, however, that now she was gone.

His legs moved towards the front part of the house, which was the only place she could be, but the redhead was nowhere to be found. Then the outhouse, but it was empty as well, then his blue eyes caught something.

Susannah.

The redhead was still dressed in her nearly-see-through white nightgown. He could see her delicate ankles and the back of her skinny thighs. She was dressed in her husband's ugly old coat and boots which he was terribly tempted to just throw away or burn.

How long had she been up? She was lucky she hadn't fainted from how weak she was.

Susannah was attempting to do two things at once. There was a shovel to take care of the snow, and currently in her hands, there was a garden plow as she was attempting to divide up the dirt in the ground even though there was a likelihood that it was going to snow again.

Why on earth was this woman so stupid? She was going to get sick again. Why was it so hard for her to stay still?

Hugh stomped towards her, trying to refrain from cursing in front of a lady, even though he'd never really cared before.

She flinched when she heard someone approach her. No doubt she was expecting a scolding.

The flush from the previous two days had already left her cheeks, but there was still a slight amount against her thin cheeks, hinting that she still had a bit of a fever.

Susannah opened her mouth, no doubt, to give him an excuse. Hugh wouldn't hear of it as he wrapped his arm around her waist until she was pressed against his side like a puppy. Susannah squirmed, but when she saw it was pointless to fight, she lay limply against his side until they were back in the cabin.

He let her up once they were inside the cabin, placing both hands on her scrawny shoulders. "What on earth is wrong with you? You're barely getting better and you're outside!"

Susannah glared at him as if he were in the wrong. He felt like he was looking at a leprechaun.

"I needed to get rid of the snow. Harry said too much snow can damage the soil—"

Hugh didn't let her finish. Instead, he scooped her up and pressed her against his side until she was facing down, with her nightgown-covered rump in the air.

His palm landed faster than she had anticipated, in the center of her cheeks.

Susannah's squeals made his dick grow hard. He briefly wondered what other sounds would come out of that sweet mouth of hers when he was on top of her.

*Calm down, Bennington,* he scolded himself as he landed another slap on her behind which was barely covered. *She's a widow for God's sake.*

A third stroke landed on her left cheek and then her right. Hugh enjoyed the way his palm dug into her soft cheeks and the way she kicked her legs.

Hugh desperately wished he could remove the thin piece of fabric and see her round, tight globes which would redden underneath his hard palm.

Alas, he needed to be a gentleman. No doubt, Mrs. Cassidy would already be angry enough at him for daring to spank her, even if she did deserve it.

His palm landed on her lower cheeks where the bottom met thigh before he decided to stop. It hadn't been a very long or thorough spanking like a grown woman who disobeyed ought to have. But Hugh had a feeling this was her first spanking. Otherwise, Susannah wouldn't be so headstrong.

Perhaps her dead husband hadn't been much of a man, after all, if he let her run around loose. Hadn't she mentioned they'd gotten married right out of the school-house? He doubted any of his brothers would have been ready for marriage at that age.

He finally placed her down again and it took every ounce

of his being not to smile as she hopped from foot to foot, trying to cool down her rear end. She glared at him ferociously, looking like she wanted to kill him. But there were no tears in her eyes.

Susannah might be flighty, but she was prideful, which was fine because Hugh had always liked a challenge.

He chewed on his bottom lip. "Stop looking at me like that. It was just a little spanking. Don't tell me you've never been spanked."

"You are a dreadful man!" Susannah spat. "How dare you spank me like a child!"

"Those were little love taps, at most, Susannah." He clicked his tongue. "A proper spanking is conducted over my knee with your bare rump in the air. If you don't want to be punished, then do as you're told."

"You're not my father or my husband; you cannot tell me what to do."

"Perhaps not, but I am your doctor, so I believe that gives me some authority over you. If you don't want me to show you what a real spanking is, I suggest you correct your tone."

She flushed then turned on her heels like the five-year-old she was pretending not to be. "I hate you!"

Hugh bit his lower lip to keep from chuckling as she locked herself in the bedroom like a child. Hugh and Susannah had only been sharing the cabin for a few days, but Susannah seemed to be on the verge of telling him that his presence was no longer welcomed.

Unluckily for her, Hugh was determined not to leave until Susannah was all better and preferably more plump that she currently was. Though he did need to contact his siblings, to let them know he was all right, as the snowstorm might have worried them. Still, he didn't want to leave Susannah alone even to go into the city to send a telegram to Larkspur Valley.

The little fool might do something even more idiotic than she had tried to do if he left her alone for too long.

If Susannah wasn't doing well by the end of the week, he would head into Laramie to send a message to his siblings and to pick up groceries. The two of them couldn't live off bread, cheese, and tea forever.

Hugh shook his head as he heard Susannah stomp her feet inside her bedroom. What was he thinking? He was acting as if he was about to move in with the woman. He needed to return to Larkspur Valley before another storm hit.

"Get some sleep, Susannah," he drawled. "You overexerted yourself this morning. We don't need your fever to be coming back."

Susannah didn't respond, but at least she stopped stomping.

Mrs. Cassidy finally emerged from the bedroom with an adorable pout on her face as she dragged herself to the kitchen table. She was probably starving after skipping breakfast and lunch due to her tantrum.

She plopped herself on the chair before letting out an adorable yelp, obviously forgetting that she still had a sore bottom. She rubbed her nates as she turned to glare at her doctor/captive. "I hope you're happy. I'm so sore, I can hardly sit down."

Hugh rolled his eyes as he pushed a bowl of soup with a piece of dry bread towards her. Susannah started shoving food in her mouth. At least her appetite had returned. "You're making a big fuss over a little spanking. I doubt they are even pink."

Susannah glared at him. She looked like she wanted to dump her soup on him.

He gave her a curt nod, letting her know that doing so would be stupid. "Just eat your dinner. If you behave like a good girl, then you have no reason to fear another spanking.

Susannah sulked for the rest of dinner even though Hugh was right. Her cheeks were only a light pink and the soreness would probably be gone by tomorrow.

"Did you think about returning to Kansas after your husband died?" he asked her again.

The question caught her by surprised. If it had been anyone else, she would have thought the question rude, but Hugh seemed to be the type who blurted out whatever was on his mind no matter if it was deemed acceptable by society or not.

"The journey from Kansas to Wyoming was terrible the first time around. I couldn't imagine doing it a second time. Besides, there was no money. There were taxes and bills to pay. And as I told you before, my parents had passed away."

"You should move to the city." Hugh pondered. "There will be better work opportunities for a woman there. You are young. You can remarry."

Susannah shook her head. She couldn't imagine marrying someone other than Harry. "I want to stay a widow forever."

It was clear Hugh didn't agree, but for the first time, he didn't press. "My offer still stands. I could help you move into the city. There are plenty of women's boardinghouses. I went to school there. I could even help you find a job. I'm sure you can sell most of the stuff here and the farm and earn quite a bit of money—"

"No, thank you," Susannah interrupted quietly as she looked at her lap. Her nightgown was so old, it was practically see-through. "I appreciate your generosity, Hugh, but I will not leave the farm."

Hugh furrowed his eyebrows at her, obviously disapproving. "Susannah, you cannot stay here. A farm is no place for a woman, let alone a single woman. If you had a son to help you—"

"Well, I don't."

"You're lucky you haven't gotten your foolish self killed." Hugh sounded exhausted. "What I am trying to say is think things through. It is only going to get harder from now on. You shouldn't be breaking your back trying to build a successful farm by yourself. You're a lady."

"I promised my husband I would stay on the farm," she whispered. "He begged me to, on his deathbed. It was his dream, Hugh."

Hugh looked angry. "Was it his dream for you to over-work yourself to death? Because that is where you are headed. There is no one around, in case there is an emergency."

"I will manage." Susannah looked at her lap while Hugh looked like he wanted to strangle her. "My husband's dream was my dream too. The winter was a rough one; it will get better once spring gets here. You'll see. Please respect my wishes."

Hugh muttered something under his breath. He obvi-ously did not agree.

"What about you?"

"What about me?"

"You are a handsome man. Don't you have a sweetheart back in Larkspur Valley?"

Susannah had tried to sound friendly, but it was obvious Hugh didn't approve of the change of conversation.

"No."

"Is there anyone you are interested in?

"Not particularly. I have no time to waste on silly girls. I've never courted anyone, and I probably never will."

Susannah looked shocked. He was so handsome, she was surprised he wasn't courting a new lady each week. Then again, his personality wasn't exactly friendly. A handsome face could only do so much.

Hugh seemed like the type to go from a cranky young man to a cranky old man whom everyone was afraid of, and he would probably die alone. It made Susannah sad at the thought, because despite his rudeness, he did have a good heart.

"Don't you want to get married? Have children?"

"And spend the rest of my life with one woman? Not particularly." He wrinkled his nose. "As for children, I have plenty of siblings. I'm sure my sisters and sisters-in-law will be popping them out by the dozen. Believe me, I will have plenty of children to look after." Hugh looked at her. "How about you?"

"What about me?"

"Your husband and you were married for a few years. You never discussed children?"

Susannah swallowed hard as she pressed a hand against her flat stomach. "It wasn't God's choice," she whispered. She didn't want to tell Hugh how much she and Harry had tried for a baby in the months before his death and how she had cried when she got her monthly.

Hugh must have sensed he hit a nerve because he didn't ask her to elaborate. He pulled out a stack of cards. "Do you know how to play Rummy?"

She nodded, an excited look on her face. "Harry taught me how to play."

Hugh grinned. "Let's play."

They played long into the night, and by the time they went to bed, she'd forgotten how sad she had been when Hugh asked her about her lack of babies.

Susannah had forgotten how nice it was to have a bit of company.

# Chapter 5

THE DAYS PASSED SLOWLY, and as much as Susannah enjoyed Hugh's company, he was driving her insane. He wouldn't let her get out of bed except for meals, he was still forcing her to do her private business in the stupid bucket, he insisted on taking her temperature rectally every four hours, and worst of all, she couldn't work on the farm.

Hugh wouldn't hear of it no matter how much she begged and whined. She finally stopped when Hugh threatened her with another spanking. One, which, in his words, would leave her sore enough that she wouldn't be able to sit down for a week.

Hugh hadn't made any additional comments about leaving and she was too embarrassed to ask him.

On the fifth day of Hugh's appearance in her life, he gave her the surprise after lunch that he was going to help remove the snow from her pathetic garden. He also offered to repair her little coop from when she and Harry had been able to afford chickens.

Susannah had begged him to be allowed to watch and he'd agreed, on the condition she only be outside for thirty minutes and that she bundle up appropriately. The minute she even sneezed, Hugh was taking her back inside.

"You're really good at this," she quipped when she saw Hugh move on from repairing the chicken coop to shoveling the snow.

Susannah had offered to help, but she had been given a death glare in response.

"I grew up my entire life on a ranch. My father was a good teacher," Hugh said with a shrug.

"You didn't want to continue ranching?" she asked curiously. Most families like the Benningtons stayed in the family business forever.

"Not really. I enjoyed it, but I've always found medicine more interesting. Out of the four brothers, Chris has always been the traditionalist, the one who wanted to continue my father and grandfather's legacy. Thankfully, the ranch is doing well enough for him to hire outside help, and my brother-in-law Finn is his right-hand man. We still help him whenever he needs help, though, especially in the summers and winters."

"The four of you seem very close." Susannah couldn't help but feel jealous. She'd always wanted siblings. Hearing Hugh talk about his family, only made her feel lonelier than before.

Hugh shrugged as if it weren't a big deal. "We're close in age. Besides, they are my brothers. I will always be there for them. My sisters too."

Susannah was about to ask him to give her advice about farming and how to get her vegetables to grow faster when Hugh surprised her by letting her know about his future plans.

"I will be leaving the day after tomorrow," he announced. "It's been almost a week since I left Larkspur Valley. The snowstorm is over and my siblings will wonder where I am.

Not to mention, I'm the town's only doctor. I must be there in case something happens. You're better now. My only advice is that you keep drinking the tea you hate so much for the next two weeks and not to overexert yourself. The last thing you want is to get pneumonia."

Susannah felt her heart drop in her chest, but she quickly recovered. Of course, he needed to return home. She mustn't be selfish, but his departure only reminded her that she would be lonely once again. Who knew when would be the next time she would have visitors.

Hugh had sent a telegram to his brother, Anthony, when he'd gone to Laramie in a hurry because he didn't want to leave Susannah alone for too long. He'd even picked up a large supply of food, making her happy. Hugh had to stop her from shoving all of the food inside her mouth when she saw him come in with the packages.

"Of course, I appreciate your generosity."

Hugh stopped shoveling snow to look at her with a serious look on his face. "I meant what I said. I think you need to leave this farm and go somewhere more civilized. A farm is no place for a single woman."

Susannah felt a pang of annoyance. Why did people insist on treating her like a porcelain doll? Her neighbors and Hugh all thought she would fail. Only Harry had believed in her. Only Harry had realized how tough she was.

"I appreciate your concern, Hugh," she tried to maintain her cheerful voice, "it will not be necessary. I will be perfectly fine handling the farm on my own. Besides, spring will be coming soon and I have all these plans—"

"Susannah," Hugh interrupted firmly, "the fact of the matter is you have no money. You do not know the first thing about farming. It is very stupid and irresponsible of you to stay here just because of a stupid promise you made to your husband."

"It was not a stupid promise." She scowled. "It was a promise made with love. I do not care if you think it's stupid. Harry and I came all this way, we made sacrifices, Harry sacrificed himself for his dream. How dare you ask me to just give it up."

"Was it your dream, or his?" he asked calmly. "Because I do not recall any woman dreaming of working and starving herself to death."

"Get out!" she scowled as she headed back into the house. "Go home! Return to Larkspur Valley and let me live my life in peace. You've done enough."

Hugh shook his head as he attempted to follow her. "You're getting hysterical, Susannah."

Susannah slammed the door in his face and locked it behind her. "I said go home, Hugh!"

Hugh pounded on the door. "Susannah!"

For a second, Susannah worried he was going to break one of the doors or windows just to spank her, but he didn't. After he finally stopped pounding on the door, she retired to her bed to cry.

No one understood how important this was to her. Hugh thought she was a fool. But then again, Hugh was judgmental enough to think everyone surrounding him was a fool.

She pressed a pillow to her chest, feeling incredibly lonely even though she'd been the one to kick Hugh out.

It was times like this, she wished she had a child to keep her company. Harry and she had tried for years, but she'd never been able to get pregnant. The one time she'd thought she was had been a false alarm. She and Harry had even saved their few pennies to visit a doctor in Laramie after the second year of not being able to conceive.

After a few embarrassing questions of both her and Harry, the doctor had confirmed that she was more than likely the infertile party. She did not always get her monthly, and when she did, it was very light. Her own mother had struggled with conceiving and hadn't had Susannah until her early forties, which she had considered a miracle. The doctor had told her it wasn't impossible she would get pregnant but that she mustn't get her hopes up.

Susannah had locked herself in her bedroom for days after, even though Harry had insisted it didn't matter if they never had a baby, as long as they had each other.

But Harry had also left her, and she had chased Hugh away. Now, she was truly alone.

Susannah must have fallen asleep at some point because when she opened her eyes, the sun was streaming through her windows. Her stomach growled as she forced herself to get breakfast.

While she waited for the bread to toast, she noticed through the corner of her eye that the barn door was slightly open. Biting her lower lip, she decided to investigate. The last thing she needed was for a wild animal to decide to make its home there.

However, when she went inside, she found that the only wild animal inside was Hugh, who was sitting across from his horse bundled up in his heavy coat.

"Hugh," she whispered. "What are you doing here? I thought you left."

Hugh opened his eyes, looking half-asleep. "You should be wearing a coat," he scolded as he stood up. "I didn't want to leave like this, with both of us screaming at each other."

Susannah gave him a pained smile. "I'm sorry for screaming at you."

"I'm sorry for being rude and trying to force my suggestions." Hugh's lip curled. It was clear, he wasn't used to apologizing. "It wasn't my place. Let's just have a normal day, Susannah. Please."

Susannah giggled. "Come inside. I'll make breakfast."

Hugh and Susannah had a quiet day. They ate breakfast, Hugh taught her how to play a new card game, Susannah helped Hugh pack and even sewed a missing button on one of his shirts. Hugh gave her some tips on farming he'd gotten from his patients, even though he clearly disapproved of her staying behind.

The next morning, Susannah gave him a packed lunch as she waited by the doorway to wish him goodbye.

"Please send a letter when you can." Susannah tried to stop her lower lip from trembling, but she was unsuccessful. "That way, I know you arrived safely."

Hugh nodded as he got on his horse. "Take care of yourself, Susannah." He paused. "I meant what I said. The second you are ready to leave this farm, send me a telegram. You have my address."

Susannah gave him a brief smile. "It won't be necessary, but thank you, Hugh. For everything."

## Chapter 6

"YOU COULD HAVE SENT the telegram earlier." Christopher scoffed as he slapped his younger brother's shoulders when Hugh made his impromptu return Sunday evening, in order to avoid going to each sibling's house to let them know he was okay. "We were worried sick,"

Hugh shrugged as he took the bowl of mashed potatoes from his little sister, Lily. Lucy was such a good cook, Christopher was sure a lucky bastard who did not deserve her. "I tried sending it as urgently as I could."

Ruby, Steve's wife, shook her head as she curled herself against Steve who was bouncing their daughter, Silver, on his knee. "I still think it's stupid you went all the way to Laramie for cigars."

Hugh raised an eyebrow. "I will gladly take back my chocolates if you don't want them." He'd gotten all of the women in his life, with the exception of Silver, a box of chocolates. Iris and Poppy had already finished half of their boxes.

Ruby stuck her tongue out. Ruby and Hugh had never

really gotten along, but now their relationship had become more sibling-like than it had been in the past.

"Well, the important thing is that you are home and this dreadful snowstorm has passed," Lucy assured him as she refilled his cup with tea.

"What took you so long, anyway?" Anthony asked, puzzled, as he rocked Lloyd, Chris and Lucy's baby, to sleep. "The storm didn't last that long."

"I stayed in the city for a few days," Hugh lied smoothly. For some reason, he didn't want to tell his siblings and sisters-in-law about Susannah. It felt too private and he didn't want to share her. Nor tell them about the days they'd shared, even though they had been completely innocent. "I wasn't sure if the storm was going to pick up again, so I thought it was safer."

Poppy hugged him tightly by the side. She'd become needy and clingy ever since she'd become pregnant. Thankfully, she had a husband to bother now and not Hugh. "Well, the good thing is you're home now. Promise me, Hugh, you'll never leave in the wintertime again."

If he hadn't left Larkspur Valley, he might have never met Susannah. Perhaps then he wouldn't be feeling this strange, hollow feeling in his chest since he had left her on her dingy, little farm.

"No promises."

Finn rolled his eyes as Poppy pouted.

Iris pulled out a stack of cards from her desk pocket. "Who wants to play?"

The cards reminded him of Susannah and how she had snorted-laughed loudly when she had finally beaten him at a card game. She had been so happy, it was almost adorable. He wondered how she was doing. Was she farming in her nightgown again? Had she gotten sick again? Was she eating properly? She'd never been good at following directions, and he imagined more so when he was not there to supervise her.

Hugh stood up. "I'm tired. I'm going home."

The days passed slowly for Hugh following his return to Larkspur Valley. He found himself feeling irritable and ill-tempered, but he wasn't sure why. Not even his medical practice, which usually brought him joy, was able to tame the negative feelings occurring within him.

More than one patient had told him that he was even ruder than usual. A fact they had come to accept because they knew he was an excellent doctor. Not even drinking, smoking, or lying with one of the local whores had been enough to cure his foul temper, something which his siblings had quickly caught on to.

Worst of all, he couldn't stop thinking about Susannah. He wondered how she was doing all by herself on that lonely farm. The idea of her getting hurt or getting sick again, this time with something worse than influenza, made his heart nearly stop inside his chest.

Susannah didn't have neighbors around her, let alone any money to pay a doctor. Before he had left, he had thought about offering her some money even though he knew she would have refused. He should have whipped her bottom if she had refused. He wondered when he had become so soft.

Susannah's face kept appearing in his dreams—nightmares might be a more appropriate word. He saw her heart-shaped face, her big green eyes, the way her red curls fell across her thin shoulders, and the thin, white nightgown which had barely hidden her charms underneath.

"Hugh, what's bothering you?" his twin, Poppy, finally asked him after Hugh invited himself to dinner at his sister and brother-in-law's home and managed to insult Finn in the process. Finn was currently taking in some fresh air outside so that he didn't end up throttling his wife's brother.

"Nothing." He lit up a cigar, even though his sister hated it when he smoked inside the house.

It was only when she put a hand on her swollen belly that he decided to put it out. Poppy was already queasy enough; he didn't want to make it worse.

"Something is obviously bothering you," Poppy pressed as she leaned forward, sniffling her little nose at him. "You haven't been the same since you returned from Laramie. You've been in an even more foul mood than usual. If you keep this up, you're going to lose all your patients. Not to mention, Finn will beat you the next time you cannot hold your foolish tongue."

"I can handle Finn," was all Hugh said.

Poppy bit her lower lip. "Did something happen? You can tell me. I won't tell anyone, not even Finn. It's just that I'm worried about you. It's been a while since you've been so unhappy."

That part was true at least. Hugh was a loner and didn't show much affection to the people in his life with the exception of his sisters, his niece and nephew, and sometimes Lucy and Ruby, when they weren't being nosy.

Hugh stared at his sister's determined face. It was possible she had grown even more headstrong since she married Finn. It wasn't surprising as Finn worshiped the ground his sister walked on and would probably let her get away with murder in exchange for a kiss.

"Do you promise you won't say anything?" he asked wryly. He couldn't believe he was confessing this to his twin who had a big mouth. But he needed to talk to someone. He needed someone to tell him that he was a fool. A fool for lusting after a stubborn woman he barely knew, and despite the few laughs they'd shared, they both equally grew irritated by each other.

Poppy nodded. "I promise. Hugh, we're twins. We can

tell each other everything. You were the first one who knew about my baby, remember? Even before Finn. Of course, you can trust me."

After he had confirmed her pregnancy, Poppy had hugged and cried for the next thirty minutes before he took her back home to her husband.

"When I was on my way back home, I was caught in a terrible snowstorm. I knew there was a possibility of being injured or dying if I didn't find shelter."

He ignored Poppy's *I-tried-to-tell-you* look.

"I found a cabin which I thought was abandoned and decided to find shelter there. It turned out, it wasn't abandoned. It was owned by a young woman, a bit younger than you. Her name is Susannah Cassidy. She's a young widow who is stupidly trying to keep the farm going because of a promise she made to her husband before he died."

Poppy managed to hide her surprise well. Hugh had to admit, he was surprised by how one woman had managed to change his moods and priorities in only a couple of days. "Is that why you stayed away for a few days?"

He shrugged. "She was sick. Starving and working herself to death for a hopeless dream. Trying to make another man who is not here happy. I asked her to reconsider living so far away from civilization and that I would help her get resettled in Laramie and help her find a job. However, Susannah is as stubborn as you. She refused to leave."

"She must have loved him very much."

"Susannah has been in Wyoming for seven years and Harry has been dead for two. She can't possibly still be missing him. Especially since, by the looks of it, he was a complete failure."

Poppy scoffed. "I think you need to work on being more sympathetic, Hugh. The woman lost her husband. She's a widow. Give her time to mourn."

"She's already mourned enough," Hugh snapped.

Poppy flinched.

Hugh ran a hand through his hair. "Sorry, Pop, I didn't mean to snap at you. These past few days—"

"You've been worried about her," Poppy finished for him, her tone gentle. "Hugh, do you feel sorry for her, or do you desire her as a woman?"

Hugh didn't answer.

Poppy let out a dry chuckle. "I'm guessing it's the latter. You are not the type to feel sorry for anyone."

"She's a widow," was all he said.

"And she has already mourned," Poppy insisted. "She's not like one of your floozies you will forget. Either you go and get her, or you leave her forever."

Hugh shook his head. "She won't come. She's too stubborn."

Poppy raised an eyebrow. "Since when are you the type to ask for permission? Just try to convince her to come to Larkspur Valley for a few weeks while she heals. You can figure out the rest of the details later."

Hugh couldn't believe he was listening to his twin sister, but early the next day, he found himself making the few days' journey to Sue's farm by horse and buggy. He felt like he couldn't get there fast enough.

Susannah was such a klutz, she was the type to trip over a branch.

He was not the type of person to believe in God even though his brother was a pastor, but he found himself praying to a God he wasn't sure existed, to make sure Susannah was safe and sound.

His heart started beating inside his chest rapidly when he finally noticed the little log cabin which indicated Susannah's home. Once he saw the barn where he had been forced to spend the night when Susannah was angry at him, he quickly commanded his horse to stop.

"Susannah!" he roared, not caring if he sounded like a lunatic.

Hugh finally noticed a small figure huddled near the entrance of the house holding a shovel and looking painfully thin despite the fact he had made sure her pantry had been stuffed with food before he left.

The dress clung to her thin body, she was practically skin and bones, and he noticed the dress she was wearing was dirty and worn out. Hugh suddenly had the desire to dress her in finer clothes to make her beauty shine through.

Her messy red hair was loose around her thin shoulders, and even from a distance, he could see how dry and red her hands were. She was probably overworking herself again.

Hugh's hands started to twitch and he suddenly had the desire to tan her hide for being disobedient. Honestly, she was like a child. Didn't she have any self-preservation skills at all?

"Hugh." Susannah's voice was soft and gentle, like a little bird.

Hugh usually wasn't into soft women. He liked strong, complicated women, women who had a rude mouth and didn't care for his own sharp tongue. Susannah was strong, but she was also overly emotional, stubborn to a fault, and the type to cry over a splinter. She could be a little fool who over-romanticized situations, yet she had been the one who wormed her way into Hugh's heart and who wouldn't leave even if she didn't notice.

Susannah dropped the shovel and walked towards him with a dazed look on her face. It was as if she couldn't believe he was real. He smiled at the thought. Perhaps she had thought of him as well.

"What are you doing here?" she asked him.

Hugh bit his tongue. He wasn't an overly emotional or needy man even though it was what women liked, to feel needed. "I was worried you'd cracked your head open while I was gone."

A soft smile appeared on her face as she pointed an index finger at her head. "Everything is where it should be." She looked amused. "Dr. Bennington, did you miss me?"

Hugh felt his cheeks grow hot, something which hadn't happened since he was a younger man. "No."

Susannah smiled like she didn't believe him. The woman was aggravating, but she was the reason why he was considering settling down like his older brothers had.

"You should be resting." He took in her sunken cheeks and the lack of color on her skin. "You look exhausted."

She gave a dainty shrug, which irritated him, as she picked up her shovel. "I am tired of resting and you can either help or stay out of my way. I really do not have time to sit and talk or be scolded, Hugh—"

Before she could finish, Hugh found himself wrapping his hands around her waist and pulling her towards him, lifting her up so their chests were pressed together.

Susannah's green eyes widened, but thankfully, she didn't pull away. Her mouth opened slightly, giving him a view of her incredible pouting lips. When he felt her wrapping her legs around his waist, he found himself growing hard and hoped she didn't notice his erection.

Susannah might be a widow, but she was still so shy, she acted like a fumbling virgin.

He could feel her hot little quim rubbing itself against the center of his stomach.

Hugh found himself holding her up by pressing each of his hands against her small buttocks before he kissed her.

The kiss was harsh, almost animalistic in nature, as he kissed her hungrily, making sure he captured every part of her sweet little lips. The redhead felt dainty in his arms and she smelled like a combination of soap and dirt.

Her hands combed his dark hair and he almost ejaculated when he felt her hands on his head. The power this woman had over him was astounding. He wasn't used to it, and for a second, he wondered if castrating himself was the solution to avoid being lovestruck, like his brothers had been for their wives.

The idea of removing his manhood quickly left his head when Susannah let out a small moan which resulted in shivers going down his body. Hugh wanted this woman. He would not rest until Susannah was his.

"Inside," she croaked.

Hugh squeezed each buttock harshly. He was only too happy to oblige.

## Chapter 7

SUSANNAH ENJOYED the feeling of Hugh's hands on her bottom even though she worried it might feel hard and bony after months of near starvation. She'd forgotten how much she adored his strong, masculine scent.

"Sue," he grunted, pulling away from her. His cheeks were flushed and his eyes were full of desire. "Are you sure?"

She nodded, feeling her nipples harden in response against her thin chemise. Since she'd been busy working in the fields, she had hardly worn underthings, including her corset, and she felt shamelessly naked.

The young woman felt like someone had possessed her and the only one she wanted was Hugh.

She hadn't realized how lonely she had felt until Hugh had come crashing into her life unexpectedly. When he left, she had thought she had lost him for good, and yet he was here now, reappearing like an angel.

Hugh pressed his thumb firmly against her chin. "I need to hear you say it, Susannah. If you want me to stop, say it now."

She closed her eyes. "I want this. I don't want you to stop."

Those sweet little words were all Hugh needed to take action. He engulfed her in another deep kiss before pulling apart the row of buttons keeping her dress firmly in place. Some of the buttons fell on the floor, earning him a glare.

His lips touched her nose. "I'll buy you another dress."

Susannah's lips felt swollen as her dress fell to the floor thanks to his roughness, leaving her in only a thin chemise and her drawers.

"Let me see those sweet little breasts," he nearly begged, his eyes fully on hers.

She gripped the sleeves on her chemise before she pulled them down, exposing the small, pale breasts with the tight, pink nipples which ached badly with need. Her pussy was bare and weeping between the slit of her drawers as she rubbed herself against his lower stomach, desperate for some friction.

"You're so beautiful," he growled as he started covering her bare breasts with bites, kisses, and slow, seductive flickers of his tongue until she was a quivering mess.

Susannah felt like she was going to faint. Her nervousness about Hugh finding her too skinny felt non-existent when she had her legs wrapped around him and he was looking at her with eyes full of adoration.

She continued rubbing herself on him like an animal in heat.

Hugh's thick rod nearly burst free from his trousers as it rubbed itself against her lower thighs. He inserted one finger inside her, chuckling. "You're so wet for me, minx."

Susannah had never liked any sort of pet name; she had even forbidden Harry from giving her one, thinking they were too silly. But when the word "minx" crossed his lips, it felt right, it even gave her a bit of pleasure that she got under Hugh's skin.

She tried to come up with something clever to say to him, but the only thing that came out were soft whimpers. Her legs were still wrapped around Hugh's torso, but she was slowly growing exhausted.

"Hugh, please."

"I'm going, minx." He dipped one finger inside her wet slit. He pulled it out, showing her how wet it was. Her cheeks burned with embarrassment. "You're so wet for me, Sue." He kissed one of her burning cheeks. "It makes you look gorgeous. Tell me, minx, have you been thinking of me?"

She nodded slowly.

"Good girl, because I've been thinking of you too." He ripped her drawers open, leaving her completely nude and vulnerable, then placed her down on the bed so he could undress himself.

Her green eyes captured every moment and every part of his body. Susannah had never looked at him closely before, but this time, she felt like she couldn't look away. She looked at his muscled chest, how curly his chest hair was, his big, muscular thighs.

Most of all, she looked at his manhood. Her mouth opened slightly when she saw the organ which would be inside her in just a few moments. The only thing Susannah could do was stare. She wondered if she hadn't acted in haste.

Hugh's member was long and thick, almost as large as one of the chair's legs. It made her wonder momentarily if she would be able to walk afterwards or if she would cry from pain. It was covered in thick purple veins and it only seemed to grow larger as Hugh gripped it with his hand.

He chuckled when he saw the stunned look on her face. "You don't need to look so frightened. I won't hurt you."

She glanced down at his cock. "I'm not worried that *you* are going to hurt me."

Hugh roared with laughter as he pulled her into a hug. She felt the warm stiffness rubbing itself against her mound. The redhead shivered with excitement. A yelp escaped her lips when Hugh slapped the right cheek of her ass, leaving behind a bright red handprint.

Susannah used her hand to rub away the sting. She glared at him. "What was that for?"

Hugh lay down on the bed, ignoring the question. He looked at her like a lazy cat, his erect cock demanding all of her attention. "Follow me." He then pointed to his twitching shaft. "Get on top of me."

"W-what?" She wasn't a virgin, but when Susannah had made love to Harry, she had always been the one on her back, not the other way around. "How?"

"Easy." He flicked his tongue. "It's like riding a horse, only my cock is your saddle." Hugh winked at her and she blushed furiously.

Susannah forced herself to approach him. She wasn't going to run away like a coward; besides, she knew Hugh would never hurt her.

"Spread your legs and get on top of me," he croaked.

She hesitated for a moment until Hugh gave her a stern look. She kneeled on the bed before she spread her thighs until she was over his protruding erection.

"Go down, minx. Slowly," he ordered through gritted teeth, his cheeks flushed.

The young woman did as she was told as her wet slit was parted open by the doctor's shaft. Her body felt warm as she accepted him inch by inch, until she was completely stuffed with his manhood.

Susannah had been wrong. It didn't hurt.

It felt wonderful.

Hugh slapped her other ass cheek, earning him a glare. He laughed, not caring if she didn't approve. "Now, ride me, Susannah. Pretend you're riding a horse."

Susannah closed her eyes and did she as he said. She began to ride him, her thighs rubbing against the sides on his hips. His cock jumped inside her, spreading her apart, deeper and deeper with each stroke.

"Good girl." Hugh started stroking her engorged clit with his thumb, causing her to buck her hips. "Faster."

Susannah moved her hips faster, her breasts and butt bouncing against her rapid movements. Her moves quickened when Hugh alternated between pinching and rubbing the little bundle of nerves between her legs.

Susannah felt so full and warm. She couldn't remember when had been the last time she had felt so wonderful. She kept moving her hips faster while Hugh played with her clit. "Hugh, I'm going to—"

Before she could finish her sentence, she felt Hugh explode inside her as his seed coated her quim and inner thighs. Her heart was beating inside her chest rapidly as she fell on top of him, feeling satisfied at having a warm body close to hers.

Susannah let out a low, small cry as he nibbled on her neck, more than likely covering her neck with marks that wouldn't leave for days. She felt Hugh breathing next to her as he rolled them over and pressed his warm body on top of hers.

The redhead had forgotten how wonderful it was to have a man on top of her again. How womanly and delicate it made her feel, especially since Hugh was twice as strong as her husband.

Hugh muttered something in her ear, but she wasn't quite sure what. Within minutes, she was fast asleep with Hugh beside her.

Susannah felt warm, which was an odd feeling in itself, since for the past few days, she had been completely freezing and huddling for warmth under the thin blankets. But today, it was different. Today, she felt warm and oddly safe, as if she were a butterfly desperately eager to get out of its cocoon. Maybe she was dreaming, or maybe spring had come early.

She jolted herself awake when she felt someone's thumb caress her breast, focusing on tweaking her pink nipple slightly.

Memories came back to her when she saw that she was fully naked and, worst of all, that a man's arm was draped over her waist. Hugh.

Her face burned with shame when she remembered how she had acted like a little harlot yesterday. How she had moaned and rubbed her body against Hugh's like a cat in heat. The way that her breasts had jiggled as she bounced herself against his manhood until they had both been screaming with pleasure. What on earth had gotten into her yesterday?

Susannah had been so happy to see him unexpectedly at her farm last night, it seemed she had lost all her senses. She shouldn't have been missing him, and she most certainly shouldn't have lain in bed with him, either.

She was a widow for God's sakes!

Susannah should have decorum and be pious, not be bedding a man because he had lovely eyes even though he had a harsh attitude.

Her poor mother would be rolling in her grave right now. And what about Harry? He would be so ashamed of her.

"Good morning," Hugh murmured as he landed a kiss on her bare shoulder. When he noticed she did not return his affections, he frowned. "What's wrong?"

Susannah turned to him, her eyes watering as she clutched the bedspread to her chest so he wouldn't see her naked.

Hugh cocked his head to the side as if he were afraid to speak. "Sue?"

Susannah burst into tears. The loud sobs caused her entire body to shake as the hot tears poured down her cheeks.

A rare, panicked look crossed Hugh's face. If she wasn't so embarrassed, she would have laughed at him. It was odd to think that such an arrogant man could be bothered by a crying woman.

"What's wrong?" he asked carefully.

The question only caused Susannah to cry harder.

"Stop it!" he hissed. "I swear, Susannah, if you don't stop crying, I will put you over my lap and give you something to truly cry about."

Susannah finally stopped crying, only to bite her lower lip. "Why are you being so mean?"

Hugh sighed. "I'm not used to dealing with crying women. Speaking of which, why are you crying? Does anything hurt?"

She shook her head. There was a little bit of blood between her thighs, though that was to be expected, she supposed. She hadn't been with another man since Harry died. It wasn't unusual that she was a little tender.

"Then why are you crying?"

"I, *we*, shouldn't have done what we did," she whispered. "It was a mistake."

Hugh clenched his jaw. "Not to me. You will never be a mistake, Susannah."

"Hugh—"

"I've been thinking about you since I left." He gripped

her small hand in his larger one. "Tell me you haven't been thinking of me as well."

Susannah gulped. "I have a husband."

Hugh looked annoyed as he let her go. "*Had*, sugar. You've been a widow for two years now. You're twenty-five. Surely, your precious husband didn't want you to remain a poor, lonely widow and take care of his dying farm as well."

Susannah flinched as if she had just been slapped. Hugh was wounded, which was why he was saying all these dreadful things. "You're being cruel and unkind."

His face softened, only slightly. "I'm sorry. It kills me that you are still sacrificing yourself for a man who is no longer in the world of the living."

The redhead shook her head. "You don't understand because you've never been married or loved someone like I loved Harry. Last night was a mistake, and we are both to blame. We shouldn't have done what is reserved only for a husband and a wife."

Hugh shook his head. He thought she was being silly, but even Hugh Bennington didn't know everything. "Then marry me."

Susannah's green eyes widened. "Pardon me?"

Hugh got up from the bed and started putting on his clothes. "If your only concern with us sharing a bed is that we are not husband and wife, then it can easily be arranged. My brother is a pastor; he can have us married as soon as we arrive in Larkspur Valley."

She looked at him, stunned. "You would marry me, just so that I can share your bed?" Susannah didn't know if she should be honored or offended. "I thought you never wanted to marry."

"I didn't." He shrugged as he looked at her with his sharp blue eyes. "Until I met you. I would marry you. I am offering to marry you now."

"I'm infertile," she whispered. Her heart dropped inside her chest as she was reminded she would once again never experience pregnancy or giving birth to Hugh's baby. "A doctor confirmed it. Harry and I tried for years and I was never able to conceive. I'm barren. I will never be able to give you a child, a family of your own."

He shook his head stubbornly. "I don't care about that. I'll have enough nieces and nephews to spoil, the way my siblings keep reproducing."

"Don't you want a family?"

Hugh gripped her by both of her arms before he kissed her. "You're my family. We can always have a litter of puppies and kittens if you want to take care of something."

Susannah gave a small smile. "Thank you, but I'm just not ready for another marriage."

Hugh's face fell. "Will you ever be ready, Sue?"

She liked it when he called her Sue. It sounded sweet. "Maybe in the future."

He nodded. "I'll take that." His lips brushed against her forehead. "But I want to make one thing clear, Susannah. Last night was not a mistake. *You* were not a mistake. Understood?"

Susannah stared at her lap, which only caused Hugh's irritation to grow. He gave her bottom a hearty slap. "I said, do you understand?"

"Yes!" She glared at him as she rubbed the buttock he had just slapped. "Do you have to be such a brute?"

Hugh laughed darkly as he began buttoning his shirt, covering his chest which was slightly covered in dark hair. "Sweetheart, you have no idea how brutish I can be."

Before Susannah could ask what he meant by that, she broke into a cough she couldn't control. It embarrassingly lasted longer than she had anticipated as Hugh flew to her side, concern written on his handsome features.

"Are you all right?"

"Perfectly." She cleared her throat. "I just need a bit of water."

Hugh shook his head, and for a second, he looked like he wanted to spank her. "You're not well. You're still ill. You probably relapsed because you haven't been taking care of yourself like I asked you to."

"I'm fine." Susannah tried to avoid his angry glare. He had the power to make her feel ridiculously small. "Coughs are normal during the winter months. Stop exaggerating, Hugh."

Hugh shook his head. "Sue, I would feel better if you had someone to keep an eye on you. I have my practice that I can't be away for long, so I think it's better—"

Susannah glared at him, her nostrils flaring. "I'm not leaving my farm!"

Hugh raised his hands in mock surrender. "Relax. I'm not asking you to leave forever, just for a few weeks. A month, at the most. I swear, I will personally return you home, but I don't like the sound of your cough and I need to make sure you are not overworking yourself to death."

Susannah hesitated. He seemed to be saying the truth. At least he wasn't planning on kidnapping and marrying her like he had thought about earlier. Besides, Hugh was right; she had been working herself to the bone, and the last thing she needed was to become a burden, especially since she didn't have anyone to take care of her.

"I can't stay with you," she said instead. "It would be improper."

"Of course. My two younger sisters live in my eldest brother's old bachelor home. They are sweet girls and Lily and Iris are away at school most of the day. My twin, Poppy, and my sister-in-law, Lucy, live nearby in case of an emergency. I live in town and will be able to check in on you

daily." He gave her a humorless smile. "Think of it as a vaca-
tion. By the time I drop you off, it will be early March and
spring will be around the corner. You won't need me then."

For some reason, his words felt like slap in the face. Did
Hugh think she was actively trying to hurt him? She was just
trying to preserve her loyalty to her dead husband. It was the
least she could do after acting like a wanton last night.

"One month," she made him promise sternly.

He nodded. "One month."

## Chapter 8

"SUSANNAH, you need to breathe. You look like you are about to vomit and I would hate to clean it up."

The remark earned him a glare from Susannah, who had been fidgeting for the last few miles of the trip. Hugh had thought that traveling by horse would give him and Susannah some much needed privacy for at least the next few days, but he had been wrong.

Susannah had been an anxious mess ever since he'd helped her sit on top of his horse Pepper and attached the little traveling bag to Pepper's saddle. Once or twice, Hugh did think she was desperate enough to crawl back home which had resulted in Hugh hardly sleeping a wink, either.

The journey hadn't been as romantic as he had anticipated, and instead, he had to watch Susannah fret as if she were meeting the Queen of England.

"Why are you so nervous?" he demanded. "You are just meeting my family."

Susannah glared at him as if he were an idiot and he was glad she had gotten back her spunky attitude. "Exactly, I am meeting your family. Do you not think they will find it strange you picked up a stray who will live with them for a month? A widow, no less." She bit her lower lip. "Maybe this was a mistake."

"This was not a mistake," he said with a shake of his head. "You are not a mistake. You are just a patient who deserves an extra pair of eyes for a few weeks. Even if my family did not attend medical school, they know how dangerous it is for a sick woman to remain alone in the middle of nowhere."

Susannah didn't look convinced, but she didn't comment. Instead, she wrapped her arms around Hugh's midsection. He felt himself going erect when he felt her hard little nipples poking against his back.

It took all of his willpower not to press her to the ground and spread her thighs apart. But since their last lovemaking attempt had ended with her crying, he assumed he should at least pretend to be a gentleman while she was staying with his family.

He would have plenty of time to convince her that it was time for her to forget about her useless ex-husband and move on to greener pastures. Specifically, on the road to becoming Mrs. Bennington.

Hugh wrinkled his nose. He wondered when he had become so mushy. His baby sister, Lily, had once accused him of being the most unromantic person on the planet, a title he had worn with pride. Now, all he wanted to do was make Susannah his wife and sell or burn the farm so she was never tempted to return home again.

When he looked at her pale face and her anxious green eyes, he wondered if she still loved her dead husband or if she just felt guilty for being young enough to want another man in her bed.

Hugh wasn't usually such a pushover and he wasn't the most patient person, but he had a feeling that if he ended up pushing too much, he would just end up driving Susannah away, something he wanted to avoid. So, for now, he had to bite his tongue.

"Is that it?"

Her quiet, little voice pulled him away from his devilish thoughts. "Is what it?"

They had arrived on a Sunday afternoon to Larkspur Valley, and instead of heading to the Benningtons' second home where Iris and Lily lived, Hugh had taken her to the Bennington's main house. It had once been the Benningtons' childhood home, but Christopher had taken over as the first born when he married Lucy.

The family had dinner together there every Sunday afternoon, since their house was the biggest. It occurred to him that having Susannah meet the entire family right off the bat might be a tad overwhelming, but it was better than smuggling her into his bachelor home in town.

A busybody would surely see and spread gossip about how Hugh Bennington was keeping a harlot in his home. The last thing he needed was for Susannah to overhear and have another meltdown. No, it was better if she stayed with his sisters, safe and sound in the country, where Hugh didn't have to think about her shy smile, bright red hair, or womanly body.

"Hugh? Did you hear me? You seem distracted."

"This is not where you will be staying," he told her as they approached the house. "This is the main house. The second house is located a few miles south, closer to town. This is my eldest brother Chris and his wife Lucy's home. They host Sunday dinner every week. I thought it would be better if you meet them before I drop you off with my baby sisters."

Her eyes bugged out comically. "The whole family? You

want me to meet your entire family in these rags?" She groaned. "Oh, I wish you would have told me, Hugh."

"You look fine," he lied. The truth of the matter was she did look pretty terrible. Even though her clothes were clean, they were thin and almost see-through from weekly washes. The one she was wearing was a faded brown color, with tiny red roses which had turned pink. Susannah had lost so much weight, it looked like she was wearing a bedspread. Her hair looked lovely, however, and it was neatly braided.

Hugh was convinced she could wear a potato sack and still look beautiful. He wanted to buy her beautiful clothes; he could afford it, after all, but he knew she was too proud to accept. Maybe he could ask his shallow sister-in-law, Ruby, to convince her. She'd always been vain.

Susannah looked miserable. "Do they know who I am? Why I am staying?"

Hugh hesitated. "Poppy does. The others will know tonight."

Susannah groaned as he helped her down. "Oh, Hugh, you should have told them. What will they think? They will probably think I'm some floozy widow who is hoping to get married again."

Hugh gave her bottom a sharp slap, causing her to squeal out in pain. "Stop it, I forbid you from acting like a poor widow. I'm a grown man and I know what I am doing. Do not worry about my family's approval. You only have to worry about mine. Are you ready?"

Susannah bit her lip, but eventually, she took the hand he was offering.

Hugh took her sweaty hand in his because he worried that if he let her go, even for a second, she would flee, although she had nowhere to go.

It was almost comical how afraid she was about meeting his family. Usually, people were afraid of him. But he knew his family wouldn't have trouble with Susannah. She was sweet, tenderhearted, and obedient when she wanted to be.

Still, he wasn't the type to bring a stranger home. A female stranger, no less, whom he had planned to let live with his baby sisters, Iris and Lily.

The dining room was filled with cheerful noises when Hugh entered the room with Susannah clutching his shirt beside him. They were just finishing Sunday dinner. Perfect.

His brothers Anthony, Christopher, and Steve were involved in a deep conversation which the saintly Anthony did not approve of if the way he was frowning was any indication. His sisters-in-law Ruby and Lucy were fussing over his pregnant twin, Poppy, who had gotten rounded and more glowing in the few short days he'd been away. Finn, his brother-in-law, was playing with their niece and nephew, Silver and Lloyd, making them laugh until they nearly choked. Iris had her nose stuck in a book, while Lily tried to get an answer from her as to whether or not bangs would suit her.

Poppy was the first to notice him as she struggled to get up from where she was. She wasn't due until May and she was already huge. Hugh worried the baby might be too big and she would have a harsh delivery. Of course, he blamed her husband for being so tall, even though Poppy wasn't exactly petite, either.

"Hugh, you're back!" She smiled as she wobbled towards them with Finn at her heels as if he worried she might trip. "Is this your friend?"

Hugh was suddenly thankful for Poppy's loud mouth because it was clear she'd told the rest of the family members what to expect. None of them looked surprised as they patiently waited for introductions.

"Yes, this is Susannah Cassidy." Hugh gently pressed a hand against Susannah's back and pushed her forward.

"It's nice to meet you, Mrs. Cassidy," Poppy said, which got rid of Susannah's shyness.

Hugh scowled when his twin called her "Mrs. Cassidy". Even though he knew he was being silly, it still irked him that another man had touched Susannah before he had. Especially since Susannah had accepted Harry's proposal and not his. He couldn't even force her to marry him, like Steve had done with Ruby, because there was little chance she could have her own biological children.

"Please call me Susannah," Susannah whispered. "You must be Poppy. Hugh has told me many things about you."

Poppy grinned as Finn placed a hand around her waist. "Good things, I hope."

"He says you are his favorite sister."

"That's not true!" Lily whined. "Hugh, you said I was the favorite!"

Iris rolled her eyes. "You're everyone's favorite because you're the baby."

"That's not true, Lloyd is the baby, at least until Poppy has her baby."

As Iris and Lily bickered, Hugh worked on introducing her to the rest of his family members. His brothers were polite to her while Ruby and Lucy fussed over her bright red hair. Lloyd and Silver just gave happy grins because they saw that everyone was happy.

Susannah was overwhelmed by the attention because she suddenly looked exhausted. It was quite clear she wasn't used to having so many people around.

Lucy must have noticed this because she placed a warm hand on their guest's shoulder. As the first one to get married to a Bennington, she was often motherly. "Susannah dear, we mustn't tire you out. Have you eaten? Would you like some dinner?"

Susannah's stomach grumbled in response. She blushed and apologized.

Ruby shook her head. "Honestly, Hugh, how do you drag her from the middle of nowhere and forget to feed her?"

Hugh glared at Ruby who he thought was a pest. He was used to going through long periods without eating. He'd honestly forgotten about Susannah since she didn't complain about being hungry. But given her malnourished form, she should probably be eating more.

Thankfully, after today, she would never suffer from hunger again.

"I didn't realize," was all he said. It was the closest thing to an apology he would give to her in front of everyone. "Eat, Susannah."

Susannah blushed as she let Lucy lead her away to a plate of warm food.

"Do you want some dinner, Hugh?" Iris asked him.

He shook his head as he ruffled her hair. "No, thank you. I'm not hungry."

"Can we interest you in a cigar?" Christopher asked casually. He rarely smoked, especially with Lucy and Lloyd at home. He knew this was just a ploy to get him to talk about what was going through his head.

Fine, he would play along.

"One cigar," Hugh warned. The last thing he needed was to spend all evening arguing with his brothers when the decision had been made. He'd brought Susannah over. The last thing he could do was throw her out in the cold. He couldn't do that to her.

Leaving Susannah distracted with the girls and Finn, he followed Anthony, Christopher, and Steve outside in the cold air.

Steve handed him and Christopher a cigar, while

Anthony refused but did help them light them. Hugh thought his brother was a saint.

He didn't smoke or drink, and he didn't gamble or swear, either. He was the perfect man to run a church. Hugh knew his sisters sometimes worried that Anthony was too preoccupied over helping others that he didn't think about helping himself and that he would never marry or start a family. As far as Hugh knew, he'd never courted anyone and he lived a celibate life. Hugh didn't envy him. It probably felt like he had the town's worries on his shoulders, yet he was still the brother everyone went to when there was trouble.

Though, sometimes he worried about what was going on in Anthony's head. Anthony was too quiet, too serene, too selfless. He was bound to explode soon. No one could remain a saint forever.

"What on earth were you thinking?" Christopher was the first to break the silence, using his big brother voice. "Bringing that girl here?"

"She's hardly a girl," Hugh scoffed. "We're only a few years apart and she's already been married."

Steve clicked his tongue. "A widow or a virgin, it doesn't matter. She's unmarried and unrelated to any of us. People will talk. They always do."

"I don't care what people say."

"You might not care, but there's a good chance she might," Anthony replied softly. "From the looks of it, she looks like a sweet girl. Sensitive."

Steve gave a loud laugh. "So, the opposite of Hugh. Marvelous. What were your plans in bringing her here? Poppy said she was ill for some time."

"She was. She is still a bit ill. Malnourished and weak." Hugh quickly told them about her dead husband and how she'd been overworking herself trying to run the farm. How when Hugh found her, she was half dead. "She doesn't have anyone nearby to take care of her and she's too stubborn to leave the farm permanently. I'm afraid she'll fall dead if I leave her alone before she gets better. I finally convinced her to come with me to Larkspur Valley for a month, so she can heal."

Steve fluttered his eyelashes. "Aw, Hugh is in love. I never thought I would see the day when you finally grew a heart."

Hugh flushed while Anthony tried his hardest not to laugh. "I'm not in love with her. I am concerned about her as a doctor. She's my patient, nothing more. I didn't want to have Sue's death on my conscience."

Steve shook his head like he didn't believe him.

Anthony raised an eyebrow. "So, it's Sue now? Do you plan on marrying her in the future?"

Hugh didn't respond.

Christopher's voice became stern. "Hugh, have you been intimate with this woman? If there is a chance you impregnated her, then you must do the right thing and marry her."

"I have. But there will be no marriage." Christopher looked like he wanted to slap him. "Susannah is infertile. She cannot have children. Besides, she has no desire to remarry; she's still pining after her dead husband. Susannah has no plans to stay in Larkspur Valley permanently, her heart is back on the farm however foolish it might be."

His three brothers looked at him with pity even though Hugh had never really wanted children in the first place. They probably thought he was a fool. He certainly felt like one, lusting after a woman who still loved her dead husband.

Christopher cleared his throat. "Perhaps it's for the best. Susannah needs time to heal from her loss and you might be happier with a woman who has no past. Someone who can give you children."

Hugh scowled. "I don't care if I ever have children. You know this."

Steve shrugged. "You might change your mind." Silver was the apple of his eye and he would commit murder for her. "You and Susannah might not be the right fit, for one thing. It's easy to confuse lust with love."

"If I recall correctly, didn't you lust after your wife before you forced her to marry you?"

Steve grinned. "Ouch. Perhaps you do feel something for this girl after all."

Christopher shook his head. "Where were you planning on having her stay, Hugh? Certainly, not in your bachelor home."

"Of course not. She wouldn't have come otherwise. I was going to have her stay with Iris and Lily. She can help with the housework while the girls are at school."

Christopher's mood darkened. "Absolutely not. I will not have a strange woman in the house with Lily and Iris, especially unprotected. We don't know anything about this woman."

Hugh crossed his arms over his chest. "She weighs a hundred pounds and nearly died of nerves just meeting you. I hardly doubt she is a serial killer."

"My answer is no, so I suggest you find another home for your little stray."

"She's not a stray. Lucy and Ruby stayed with the girls before you married them. Why is this any different? We hardly knew them at the time, either."

"It's different because we planned on marrying them. What you and Susannah have is complicated."

Anthony must have sensed the brothers were close to fighting because he spoke up. "How about we ask Lily and Iris if they are comfortable with Susannah staying there? I'm sure Hugh or I can check in on them throughout the day and it's only for a few weeks after all."

Hugh threw a grateful look at Anthony. Finally, someone

with sense and non-judgment. Which wasn't surprising, as he was the one who always welcomed the new members with open arms while his brothers were more suspicious.

Christopher looked tired, while Steve was amused. "Fine, but if either Lily or Iris say no, then, Hugh, you are paying for an inn for her or taking her back to her farm."

Unsurprisingly, Lily and Iris agreed to have Susannah stay with them. Susannah spent nearly an hour thanking them with her head bowed and her cheeks flushed.

As Hugh watched her, he hoped he hadn't made a mistake in allowing her to be so close to his life.

---

The days flew by for Susannah Cassidy, and before she knew it, a whole week had passed. She thought it would be awkward living with Hugh's sisters, but Lily and Iris were actually very sweet.

She'd taken over most of the household chores such as the cooking and the cleaning, since Iris and Lily were at school for most of the day. Susannah actually found the tasks refreshing. It was nice to cook and clean with a full belly, a full pantry, and money for whatever else she needed.

Susannah had forgotten how nice it was to live in a full house filled with laughter and joy. She envied the Benningtons for having such a close-knit family. The older Benningtons visited often. She had a feeling Christopher Bennington didn't fully trust her and she didn't blame him; she was a stranger after all, but by the end of the week, he'd seemed to have warmed up to her.

Hugh visited often for dinner with the excuse that he was coming to see how she was feeling. He often stayed behind, to talk to the girls or play a game with them until it became too late and he had to return to town.

"How were your patients today?" Susannah asked one night after dinner while she walked him to the porch. Her heart felt heavy inside her chest every time he left, as if it wanted her to beg him to stay.

Hugh shrugged as he gave her a twenty-minute recap on the nail he had to remove from a farmer's wife who accidentally stepped on it.

"Which is why when you are outside, it's important to always wear shoes. You never know when you may step on something which can easily turn into an infection." He stopped rambling when he noticed she stood there with a slight smile on her face. "What is it? You're staring."

"Nothing." Susannah smiled. "I'm just very grateful you found me a place to stay. I will be sad to leave in three weeks. I've gotten used to having people around."

Hugh didn't look pleased by her reminder that she was due to leave soon. "I'll come check on you tomorrow." He patted her cheek and she nuzzled it against his large, warm hand. "Be good, please."

Susannah gave him a cheeky smile. "I always am."

The next day was Saturday and, in Susannah's world, wash day. Since Iris was busy studying, she roped Lily into helping her wash this week's clothes and bedding.

Lily was a pretty, joyful little thing and she would no doubt be the talk of the town once she grew older. She reminded Susannah of the sun—warm, bright, and cheery. Even Hugh wasn't cranky when he was around her.

"Do you really live on a little farm all by yourself?" Lily asked as she placed the dresses in the wash tin.

Susannah was beside her, scrubbing the dirt off one of Lily's school dresses. "I do. I've lived there for seven years, since my husband and I got married. I live there on my own now."

Lily's blue eyes widened comically. "By yourself? Don't

you get lonely?"

Susannah gave a hollow laugh. "Sometimes, but I like the quiet. It can be pleasant as well. I never did want to live in a city. It's too loud and crowded. I grew up living in a little town like Larkspur Valley."

Lily pursed her lips. "Well, I want to live in a big city like New York. It would be so exciting and loud. There will be so many things to do and places to explore." She sighed dramatically. "Larkspur Valley is so boring. There is nothing to do. I don't want to keep house like Lucy, Ruby, and Poppy, at least not now. I want to explore." She sighed. "But my big brothers would never let me leave. They baby me too much. They think anything outside Larkspur Valley is dangerous."

"Well, you are the baby of the family." Susannah laughed as she teasingly pinched Lily's cheek.

Lily scowled. "I can take care of myself. Besides, the world is changing. It's 1873 and women have more independence than ever before."

Susannah chuckled gently. "The world is changing, Lily. Rapidly. Don't fret. Just focus on finishing school. You never know, your brothers might change their minds when you're older. It's only a matter of time before we are surrounded by cities. Traveling by train has made going someplace new so convenient."

Lily looked doubtful and the redhead didn't blame her. Christopher ruled the Benningtons with an iron fist, and while Lily was still young, she could be flighty. "From your lips to God's ears." She hugged her knees to her chest. "So, are you really leaving in three weeks?"

"I am. I was sick for a long time. Hugh was worried I would get worse if I stayed on the farm by myself."

"Oh, I thought Hugh brought you here to make you his wife and that you were only staying with us until Anthony could marry you off."

Susannah reddened. Why did everyone think she was a bride-to-be? "I'm not getting married anytime soon, Lily. I'm still mourning my husband."

The blonde looked at her with pity. "I understand."

Then because neither of them knew what else to say, they finished the washing in silence. After they were finished, Anthony came over to pick up Lily because she was meeting a friend in town, leaving Susannah alone with Iris.

Susannah knitted quietly while Iris flipped through a history book the size of her head. There was an intense look on her pretty face, making her look older than she was. There were crumpled pieces of paper around her. It was obvious she was under a lot of stress.

Susannah cleared her throat. "Hugh told me you want to be a teacher."

Iris nodded, not bothering to look up from her book. "I graduate from school in May, take the teaching examination in June, and hopefully secure a teaching spot in Larkspur Valley." She sighed irritably. "My brothers refuse to let me leave, even though I will already be eighteen. Not to mention, the town only has one school and the school board has never hired a woman teacher. They are being pigheaded."

"I'm sure they will change their mind in a year or two." Susannah looked at her with sympathy. She couldn't blame Hugh, Christopher, and Steve for not allowing Iris to leave on her own, even for a job. She was slight, pretty, and although she was book smart, she was obviously very sheltered, which wasn't always the best combination for a woman traveling on her own.

Iris sighed. "I doubt it."

"Just concentrate on finishing school and passing your teaching exam. I promise I will speak to Hugh before I leave and try to convince him to let you teach elsewhere. If you have one brother on your side, I'm sure it will go well."

Iris smiled, although it was clear she didn't think Susannah would be able to do much convincing.

"I was a teacher once too. Before I married obviously. Only for a year."

Iris raised an eyebrow. "Really? Hugh didn't mention anything."

"It was such a small part of my life, I suppose it is why I don't mention it often," she admitted. "But I did teach for one year at my old one room schoolhouse so I could help Harry, my husband, to save money so we could afford to move to Wyoming."

"Did you enjoy it?"

"I did. The children were very sweet. Though I do admit, I didn't enjoy teaching arithmetic."

Iris smiled. "Do you ever miss it?"

"I must admit, I like being around the children, more than actually teaching. I always wanted to be a wife and mother, so I didn't mind leaving that much because, eventually, I knew I would have my family." Susannah's voice broke, reminding her she would never carry her own baby in her womb. "But your reasons might be different."

Iris pondered on this. "I wish I didn't have to choose between having a career and a family. But since I do, I chose teaching. I've been wanting to teach since I was five years old. Also, I'm sorry you lost your husband."

Before she could thank her, the door burst open and a very pregnant Poppy stormed in. She was still riding the new pony Finn had gotten her as a present for when she got pregnant even though he had warned her more than once that he would spank her if she continued riding before she gave birth. Poppy didn't seem to care and continued riding her pony everywhere.

"Hello, I thought I would come help start dinner."

"Shouldn't you eat at your own house?" Iris asked, annoyed that she and Susannah's conversation had been interrupted.

She shrugged. "I told Finn we would eat here today."

"Does your precious Finn know you rode your pony here? Do you want to have your baby early?"

Poppy's cheeks pinkened slightly. "Oh, Iris, go upstairs and take a nap. All this studying is making you cranky. I am perfectly equipped to help Susannah with dinner."

Iris murmured something under her breath but did as she was told. It was clear Poppy was the mother hen around here, even if she was married and had her own household. It amazed Susannah that she and Hugh were twins and they had such different personalities, though they both shared the same temper.

Poppy placed a hand on her large belly. "I was thinking of fried chicken for dinner, what do you think? I brought a plucked hen from home and it should be enough for the six of us. Hugh usually joins you girls for dinner, doesn't he?"

She nodded. Hugh joined them for dinner nearly every day, unless he was busy with a patient. During dinner, he didn't talk much and only seemed to stare at her as if he couldn't believe he'd actually dragged her away from her farm. It wasn't like they could talk in private like they used to, since his little sisters were around. Not to mention, Susannah had a feeling Hugh was still a little annoyed over his rejected marriage proposal.

Susannah and Poppy worked quietly on dinner until Poppy spoke up while holding a raw chicken thigh. "Susannah, do you love my brother?"

She nearly dropped the vegetables she was chopping into fine pieces. "W-what?"

"I asked if you love my brother?" she asked quietly. "It's

not every day Hugh brings a girl to live here, even if she's a patient. You're the first girl he has shown interest in courting properly."

Susannah hesitated, unsure of what to say. Poppy was in love with her husband; she wouldn't understand how terrible it was to lose someone she loved. Even if she had lost her parents, it wasn't the same thing as losing a lover.

"I've told Hugh I am not ready to court after my husband's death. I am not sure if I ever want to marry again. He is aware of my feelings."

"So, you feel nothing for him?"

Susannah blushed. "I care for him, but I don't think I want to marry. At least not now."

Poppy nodded as she started cutting the chicken breast into smaller pieces. "Well, I sure hope you tell Hugh that, because he keeps looking at you as if you're a glass of water in the desert." She stopped cutting. "You seem like a sweet girl, Sue. I don't mean to be blunt, but I don't want to see my brother get hurt. The longer you stay here, the harder it will be for him to move on."

After her conversation with Poppy, Susannah was unusually quiet during the rest of the evening, even though she always tried her best to add to the conversation and enjoyed the jokes everyone told at the dinner table.

Susannah excused herself after dinner, to sit on the porch outside while the Bennington sisters and Finn argued about something they'd read about in the newspaper. She sighed as she looked at the stars glowing above her. Today had been a strange day and she'd been given a lot of things to think about.

"Are you all right? You were quiet in there." Hugh sat next to her and she took in his masculine scent. He always smelled of grass and cigar smoke. It had a pleasant scent.

"Yes, I'm all right. Your sisters just got me thinking about all kinds of things today."

Hugh scowled. "Were they rude to you? Don't listen to them; they have big mouths."

Susannah shook her head. "Nothing like that. The three of them are very sweet. Iris reminded me of my teaching days."

"I didn't know you taught."

"Yes, for a year, in order to save money to move to Wyoming. I enjoyed it for the time I did it, but it wasn't what I wanted to do for the rest of my life. I left it all to marry Harry, and because to me, raising a family was my biggest dream." Tears pooled at her eyes as her chin wobbled. "And now, I see you and your big, wonderful family and I can't help but be jealous that I will never be able to experience that. I will never have a full dinner table on Sundays or grandchildren to spoil. I will never have children of my own or watch them grow up. My womb will always feel empty." Tears fell down her cheeks. "I want a baby sometimes so badly it hurts. Why can't I be a mother?"

Hugh hugged her close to his chest and attempted to comfort her by rubbing her back while she sobbed, splashing his shirt with her tears. He let her cry for a few minutes, not speaking. He knew there was nothing he could say to make her feel better. He couldn't promise her a baby. Instead, he let her cry until her body was limp with tiredness.

"Having a big family isn't all it's cracked up to be," Hugh grumbled as he rested his chin on top of her head. "They can be pretty darn annoying as well."

Susannah laughed as she allowed herself to snuggle against Hugh. She knew in his own, detached way, Hugh was trying his best to make her feel better, and for that, Susannah was grateful.

# Chapter 9

AFTER HER MELTDOWN—SUSANNAH wasn't sure what she could call it exactly—things in her life calmed down significantly. She had a routine she followed every morning after Lily and Iris went to school.

Chores and cooking kept her busy so she wasn't constantly lost in her own head, but Hugh must have felt some sort of pity towards her, because his sister and Lucy or Ruby stopped by more often in the mornings so she wouldn't feel lonely. Sometimes Hugh dropped them off, or other times, their husbands did.

Susannah appreciated the company. The four of them were around the same age and got along splendidly. Susannah often felt like a young schoolgirl again, instead of a dowdy widow, when she was around them.

"It's Hugh and Poppy's birthday next week," Lucy mused one morning when it was just her and Ruby. Poppy was conveniently absent since her feet had been swollen for a few days and Hugh recommended bed rest, something which made her unhappy.

"We should do something." Ruby watched as her daughter, Silver, forced baby Lloyd to play with dolls with her even though the happy baby did nothing more than stuff the rag doll in his mouth. "We haven't done anything big since Christmas. What about a party?"

Lucy hesitated. "Poppy needs to rest more, Finn tells me she's on her feet more often than not. If we plan a party, she will want to meddle like she always does. Not to mention, Hugh is not a big fan of parties; he wouldn't want strangers here to make small talk on their birthday. Maybe we should do a simple dinner with just the family, with foods they both like and a cake, of course."

Ruby pouted. "Fine. But when it's my birthday, I expect a bigger celebration than that."

"Your birthday was in January."

"And I was sick with a fever. It doesn't count. I wish my birthday was in the summer."

Susannah spoke up. "Hugh doesn't like cake. He doesn't like sweets too much."

Both women turned to stare at her. She blushed.

"He mentioned it in passing. But he likes popcorn, I'm sure we can purchase some corn to make some and salt it."

Lucy smiled at her. "What a fantastic idea. Between the two of us, Susannah, we can do a roast and maybe some fried chicken. I have some strawberry preserves left. I can make a vanilla cake and place them on top for Poppy, to make it extra sweet. We can make it a surprise party for both of them. Otherwise, Poppy will try to meddle and she can't risk the baby coming early."

Ruby placed her hands on her narrow hips. "What am I supposed to do?"

Susannah and Lucy exchange glances. Ruby was a notoriously bad cook, even though Poppy and Lucy had tried to teach her since she married Steve. Ruby either burnt everything she touched or served it raw.

A smile appeared on her lips. "I'm kidding. I don't want to poison anyone at a birthday party. I can help Iris and Lily with the decorations."

"Mama!" Silver raised her hands, which were covered in sugar because of one of the cookies Susannah had given her.

Ruby picked her up and kissed her cheek loudly. "What do you think, Silver? Should we make a birthday card for your grumpy aunt and uncle?" Lloyd crawled behind her and smiled, showing two bottom teeth. "You can help too, Lloyd."

The days went flying by as Susannah helped Lucy with the preparations for Poppy and Hugh's birthday dinner the following Saturday. As she distributed her time between prepping the food and helping Iris and Lily make decorations, she wondered worriedly what the perfect present for Hugh might be.

The man had saved her life, after all, and he gave her a roof over her head while she recuperated, even though she didn't have a penny to her name.

A pair of knitted socks or scarf didn't seem like a nice present. Besides, Lucy was an expert with a needle and thread and often sewed or knitted things for the Benningtons. Her own pathetic attempts paled in comparison.

In the end, she asked his sisters for help. Iris had suggested a new medical textbook since those were the only things he enjoyed reading, while Lily suggested something to decorate his medical office. She chose the second option.

As much as she would love to give him a textbook, she only had a handful of pennies to her name. Lily was generous enough to share her watercolors with her.

She painted a small landscape portrait of Larkspur Valley for him to hang it in his office while she made Poppy a painting for her baby's nursery, filled with poppies, larkspur flowers, baby chicks, and cows.

It wasn't her best attempt, but Susannah didn't have many talents. She just hoped the twins liked them as she placed a large red bow on each of them.

---

"They're coming!" Lily said to the rest of the Benningtons, their wives, and Susannah, who had shown up earlier, to finish decorating and to hide before the twins came.

Finn was helping a pregnant Poppy out of the wagon. She'd gotten heavier in the past few weeks. Finn was worried they were having twins, though Hugh insisted he only heard one heartbeat and felt one baby kick. Hugh followed lazily behind them.

Susannah blushed as she looked at his gray trousers and matching vest and she couldn't help but notice that he looked extremely handsome today.

Memories flowed in of when she and Hugh had made love—how his large, strong hand had squeezed her buttocks and the way he had filled her with his manhood. Susannah hated to admit that she missed his touch. A spanking even seemed welcome right now. She had to pinch her cheeks to prevent herself from acting like a fool.

"Surprise!" they screamed as Hugh and Poppy entered the room.

Poppy squealed in delight as she started hugging her sisters. Taking advantage that all eyes were on Poppy, Susannah approached Hugh shyly with her gift. "Happy twenty-eighth birthday." She held up the painting. "I'm sorry it isn't much, but I hope you like it."

Hugh took the painting with surprising gentleness. "Larkspur Valley. For my office?"

She nodded shyly, unsure of what else to say, especially with everyone else in the room.

Hugh cupped her cheek and she was sure her entire body was as red as her hair. Lily burst out laughing before she gave her a wink of encouragement.

"Thank you, Sue. My sisters are always complaining that it is too bare in my office. Now they finally have nothing to complain about."

Lucy squeezed her shoulder gently. "Sorry to interrupt but, Susannah dear, will you help me serve dinner? I have Ruby and Iris helping me with the babies."

Susannah nodded as she followed Lucy, avoiding Hugh's warm gaze on her. She could tell he wanted to say something else, but she wasn't sure she was ready to hear what those things were.

After dinner, they had birthday cake and popcorn, and while Poppy forced them to play a game of charades, Hugh discreetly went outside to smoke his after-dinner cigar since Lucy and Ruby didn't like him smoking around the kids.

He let out a puff of smoke as he leaned against the door-way. Hugh usually didn't care too much about birthdays, but he thought this one wasn't bad at all. He especially couldn't stop thinking about the birthday gift he received from Susannah and her shy expression.

She could be quite adorable when she wasn't being stubborn.

When he heard the front door creak open, he turned around to stare at his baby brother. "What are you doing here?"

Anthony smiled sheepishly as he rubbed the back of his neck. "Poppy kicked me out of charades. She said I was too terrible to play. Can I join you?"

"Only if you don't complain about me smoking."

Anthony joined him, closing the door behind himself. The next words he said surprised Hugh. "You need to marry that girl."

He raised an eyebrow. "Excuse me?"

Anthony rarely got involved in other people's lives and knew how to bite his tongue, which was why his comment surprised Hugh.

"Susannah," he clarified, "you need to marry Susannah."

Hugh raised an eyebrow. "Since when did you turn into a matchmaker?"

Anthony had the decency to look embarrassed. "I see the way you look at her. You've never looked at another lady like you do her. She's very sweet and she brings out the best in you. You are more patient and kind when she's around. I know she's a widow, but even the church encourages widows to marry again. Everyone needs a partner." His voice softened. "I wouldn't want you to lose her because you're afraid of being honest with your feelings."

"She's in mourning. Susannah won't marry anyone." Hugh's voice was cold. Anthony looked like he regretted bringing it up. "There's no point in hoping something else will happen. Maybe you should stop thinking about me and focus on finding your own wife."

His words stung as Anthony murmured an apology. He knew he wasn't being fair. His brother only had his best interest at heart after all.

But the truth of the matter was Susannah had already rejected his marriage proposal once. Even if she changed her mind, Hugh wasn't sure he would be a good husband. He was too selfish and stubborn, something women rarely enjoyed.

No, it was better this way. Then Susannah and he could both avoid being disappointed.

"Are you sure you will be all right on your own?" Anthony asked worriedly a week after Hugh and Poppy's party, as he helped Susannah out of the wagon. Hugh had sent a curt message out of the blue via Anthony that he wanted to see her this morning for her checkup.

The loud coughs had diminished greatly and she had even gained a healthy amount of weight. Her clothes no longer looked loose and misshapen as if she were wearing a pair of sheets. Dare she say she even looked pretty.

Sweet Lily had even commented that her new pink cheeks matched her flaming red hair.

"It's a long walk back to the house, especially in these freezing temperatures. If my brother can't take you back, stop by the church and I will take you."

"Thank you, Anthony, that is very kind of you."

Anthony blushed as he waved goodbye, leaving Susannah in front of Hugh's clinic where he spent the majority of his time.

It was a large brick building, with a simple white plaque which read, *Dr. Hugh Bennington*.

Susannah shifted uncomfortably in her dress, not sure what to do. It felt like ages since she had spoken with Hugh even if, in reality, it had only been a week. Things had been tense between them since the birthday party and she had decided to give him some well-needed space, though it was a bit lonely. She had gotten used to his company and his dry humor. He hadn't even come for dinner at all this week, claiming he was too busy.

Susannah understood. Still, he could have told her himself that he wanted to perform a checkup on her, instead of sending poor Anthony, who looked like he hated being stuck in the middle.

Before she could continue being lost in her own head, the front door opened and Hugh stepped forward, looking annoyed. "Are you just going to stand there all day, or are you actually going to come in?" he barked cruelly.

Susannah jumped as she bit her lower lip. "Sorry, I was just looking at the building—"

"There's nothing special about it," he said curtly as he nearly pushed her inside the clinic. "You're acting like you want to get sick. Again."

"You don't have to be so rude!" she growled.

Hugh didn't apologize, but his grip around her arm softened a bit as he led her to a small bed at the end of the hallway.

Her eyes widened when she saw her painting on one of the walls. She smiled. "You kept the painting."

She didn't know why, but the fact he kept her painting made her smile, especially since he had been so rude lately.

"I needed something there," he added absentmindedly as he pulled out the stethoscope. "Now, no talking, I need to concentrate."

Susannah did as she was told and he quickly examined her. Thankfully, he didn't ask her to take her clothes off.

"You've put on weight." Hugh looked pleased. "Amazing what three meals a day will do to you. Hopefully, you'll remember that when you're surviving on grass and acorns once you return to the farm you are stubbornly clinging too.

His words stung and Susannah felt like she had been slapped. "You're being mean," she accused quietly. "Not just today, but since your birthday party, you've been a real arse, and I want to know why."

Hugh's jaw clenched as he narrowed his eyes on her. He looked like he wanted to spank her, and even though she didn't fancy being over his lap again, she also didn't want him to walk all over her.

"Maybe you're being overly sensitive, Mrs. Cassidy."

She raised a red eyebrow. "Mrs. Cassidy? What happened to Sue?"

"You keep reminding me that you were married and your loyalty remains with your husband, so I thought you would prefer being addressed by your married name,"

She shook her head. Hugh accused her of being childish, but truth be told, he wasn't much better. "You're being ridiculous. It is because I care about you, Hugh, that I am being honest with you. I want to save you from any unnecessary pain." She took a deep breath. "If I would have met you first, things would have been different. If I had never married Harry or had the farm, I would have chosen you in a heartbeat."

Hugh gripped her shoulders firmly, forcing her to stare at him. "Stop living in the past. He is dead and I'm here, and I would do anything for you, Susannah."

"I know you would, but—"

Hugh didn't let her finish. Instead, he pulled her in for a deep kiss with his hands resting around her waist. At first, she tried to fight the kiss, but his lips felt so good.

It had been too long since she had kissed Hugh. She had forgotten what a good kisser he was and how wonderful his lips felt when they were kissing her so passionately.

Susannah wanted to tell him to stop, to pull away. She needed to remain loyal to her husband, after all, but she was like a woman possessed, unable to stop.

Hugh kissed her as if he was never going to kiss another woman again. It made her feel oddly possessive of him. Especially since she knew for a fact that he had never courted anyone properly before.

His large hand tugged at her red hair, not painfully, but definitely firmly. "Last chance," he croaked. "If you want me to stop, tell me now."

"I don't want you to stop," she whimpered. She could feel her nipples painfully erect under her corset. "Don't stop."

She couldn't believe the words coming out of her mouth, but they were true, no matter how horrified she was of them. Susannah wanted Hugh. She wanted every part of him.

Those were the only words Hugh needed to start unbuttoning the front part of her dress rapidly. He let out a series of curse words when he struggled with the last two buttons. She could see his erection pressing painfully against his trousers and he wanted to let it lose.

Finally losing his patience, he pulled apart the thin fabric harshly, causing the last two buttons to fall to the floor and for the material to be torn in half, leaving her with bare shoulders and just her underthings beneath.

"Hugh!" she snarled. "I don't exactly have a closet full of dresses like your sisters."

"I'll buy you another one." Hugh kissed her quickly in an attempt to pacify her anger. It worked, as her expression softened. "I'll buy you as many dresses as you want, but please let me continue kissing you, Sue."

The anger dissolved as quickly as it appeared while she allowed him to kiss her as he fumbled with her remaining clothes until they were a pile on the floor.

It didn't feel strange being nude in front of Hugh. Perhaps it was because he was a doctor or because she felt beautiful around him, but her nakedness didn't bother her. Dare she say, she felt beautiful.

When Harry had still been alive, she had often felt shy and insisted on making love only at night, which Harry had obliged. Now, here she was, having extra-marital relations with a man who was not her husband, in broad daylight.

Her worries were pushed away as Hugh squeezed one of her breasts, his thumb brushing against the tight, peach-colored nipple.

Susannah whimpered but didn't push him away. Instead, she arched her chest forward as she begged for more.

Hugh dutifully played with her breasts, squeezing them gently, pinching her nipples, and giving them little kisses when she whined that he was biting too hard.

"Hugh." Susannah cupped his manhood in her hands, enjoying how heavy it felt. "Please."

"Please, what?"

She squeezed his balls through his trousers, enjoying the way his cock jumped in her hand. "Please fuck me."

Hugh kissed her so hard, she was afraid she was going to bruise. He pressed her against the small patient bed until her breasts were on the mattress and her bottom was in the air.

Four slaps landed on her upturned rear, covering her with lovely pink handprints. Another three slaps echoed in the room. She cried out in pain, but she wasn't a fool. She recognized the familiar throbbing sensation between her legs, indicating to her that she didn't mind being spanked too much.

"I should spank you," Hugh growled in her ear as he parted her legs open with his thigh. His hand landed in the center of her wet quim. He rubbed the sting away, his fingers on her entrance only making her more wet. "You've been denying me for weeks, Sue, when you've wanted this all along, haven't you?"

Susannah let out a small little moan, but she was too embarrassed to look at him.

He gripped her bright red hair in his hand. "Answer me, Susannah. Have you wanted me as much as I wanted you?" He pulled on her hair even more tightly. "Careful. I know when you're lying and I have no problem stopping and belting your ass bright red if you decide this is a good time to fib."

"I've wanted you since the first day I saw you." Susannah's voice was quiet and she was surprised by how quickly the guilt left when she saw Hugh's expression soften. It looked gentle and warm.

"There's my girl."

Hugh gripped her by the hips and pounded into her in one quick, swift motion which caused her mouth to open in surprise while her legs trembled. Her wet, pink quim stretched itself around his cock, trying its best to accommodate him.

Unfortunately for her, Hugh wasn't at all patient today. It seemed he was determined to make her his by burying himself as far as he could inside her even when she was struggling to accept him. It had been a while since they'd made love after all.

Hugh's fingers gripped her hips as her bottom slapped his lower belly with each stroke which nearly split her apart. Their bodies connected as one as he filled her over and over again with his manhood.

Susannah's clit rubbed against the edge of the mattress each time he pulled out, only to bury himself inside her again as the room was filled with skin slapping against skin. It felt so wonderful having Hugh inside her.

It was nice being reminded she was not only just a widow, but a woman as well. Especially while Hugh made love to her dominantly, as if reminding her that he had the final word about everything. Susannah closed her eyes in pleasure as she felt him finish inside her, his hot seed dribbling down her inner thighs. She rested her cheek exhaustedly against the mattress, feeling completely satisfied.

"Hugh." Susannah looked over her shoulder. Her ass was bright red from his earlier spanks and the way he had gripped her ass during sex.

Hugh rubbed some of his leftover cum which had dripped down her thigh on her butt. "Yes, Sue?"

"Anthony can't give me a ride home like this. I'm half naked."

Hugh barked a laugh. "Don't worry, honey. I won't let anyone see you like this. Not even my brother the pastor. I'll take you home."

Home.

Since she'd married Harry, home had been the farm, but now her views had shifted. The farm, as lovely as it was, was starting to look a bit lonely to her, as if it were missing something.

Hugh.

## Chapter 10

MARCH QUICKLY CAME and before Susannah knew it, she had lived with the Benningtons for exactly one month. All traces from her illness last winter had been erased and she couldn't remember the last time she had felt so healthy.

Hugh had promised her she could leave after one month and Susannah's feet itched to go back to her little farm. As much as she enjoyed her time with the Benningtons, it would be nice to return to the quietness of the country without someone monitoring her constant movements and reporting them to Hugh. Though, if she were being honest, the main reason she wanted to return home was to avoid the awkwardness which had once again transpired between her and Hugh after they made love in his clinic two weeks ago.

Even after Susannah had sworn she would never again fall into his arms or make love to him, it seemed she lost her senses whenever Hugh was around. She was a fool. A traitor. A bad wife, who was lusting after a man so soon after her husband's death.

Hugh must have sensed her guilt and regret even though she had begged him to make love to her, because Susannah had hardly seen him these past two weeks, and when she did, it was just cold interactions. It amazed her that Hugh could make love to her so tenderly one moment and then treat her coldly the next, though she could hardly blame him. She wasn't treating him very nicely in the first place. Susannah wasn't usually the type of girl to play with a man's feelings, especially a man who had treated her so tenderly when that wasn't usually how he acted.

Susannah sighed. She was so confused. She didn't know what to say or how to behave anymore. All she knew was she wanted to make things better with Hugh before she departed.

She appreciated the Benningtons' generosity and kindness, but she couldn't live on their pity forever. Besides, she shuddered when she thought about the farm. There were probably weeds everywhere, not to mention gophers and squirrels popping up wanting to eat everything in sight.

Susannah had asked Anthony, the most approachable of the Bennington brothers, if he would be able to give her a ride back to her farm.

Anthony had simply raised an eyebrow and asked her if Hugh had given her permission to return, which annoyed her to no end. Why did everyone insist on acting as if Hugh owned her or had some almighty power over her? They weren't married, even if they had become close like husband and wife.

She had a feeling no one would contradict Hugh even if it was obvious she was well enough to go home and take care of herself. She had discussed her dilemma with the other women and they were sympathetic. They had no idea that Susannah and Hugh had been intimate. Even though she wanted to share the news with someone, she was too ashamed to admit it.

Ruby had suggested Susannah pretty herself before

Sunday dinner, so she could convince Hugh it was time to let go.

She borrowed a dress from Poppy which didn't fit anymore due to her pregnancy, a pretty blue dress with tiny daisies.

Lily had even helped her arrange her hair because she was too clumsy to do it herself. Lily was all smiles as she made Susannah twirl around to show off her dress and hair. "You look beautiful! Like a princess!"

Iris crossed her arms over her ample chest. "Hopefully, it will be enough to convince Hugh to let you leave. He can be a stubborn ass."

Susannah blushed at the swear word.

Lily pouted. "I don't want you to leave, Sue. I like having you here. You're much more fun than Iris."

Iris scowled as she pinched her sister on the ear.

Not wanting to get involved in their squabbling, Susannah told them they should probably check on dinner.

Usually, Christopher and Lucy hosted Sunday dinner, but she had asked them if she could do it this week as a farewell dinner. They'd agreed even though they expressed doubts over Sue leaving so soon.

Susannah was determined to leave. Hugh had promised she only had to stay for a month and she had done her time.

With Iris and Lily's help, they had made pot roast, roasted vegetables, mashed potatoes, and bread rolls. Iris had even managed to make a pecan pie at the last minute.

"This is delicious, Sue." Ruby took a second helping of mashed potatoes. "You're an excellent cook."

"Iris and Lily helped me a lot," Susannah answered modestly.

"You think everyone who doesn't burn food like you is a good cook," Steve teased his wife as he playfully bumped her shoulder.

Ruby rolled her eyes as she squeezed her husband's thigh.

Susannah looked up expectantly at Hugh, but he didn't say anything. Instead, the man kept shoving food inside his mouth as if he hadn't eaten in days. There had been a grouchy expression on his face since he arrived for dinner that didn't exactly make him approachable.

Poppy said she shouldn't worry, as he was often cranky.

Sensing Susannah's desperation, Lucy cleared her throat. "How about after dinner, we play a nice game of charades? Won't that be fun?"

The men groaned. Lucy responded by kicking her husband's knee.

Christopher shook his head as if he could sense what was going on in Hugh's head. No one could force Hugh to do something he didn't want to do.

They finished dinner then dessert quickly. Afterwards, the women forced everyone to the sitting area, with the exception of Hugh, who excused himself to smoke.

Leaving the dinner dishes behind, Susannah went after him. She stepped outside nervously. "May I join you?"

He grunted in response, but at least he wasn't scowling at her like he usually was. "How are you?" she asked awkwardly.

"Is this really what you want to ask?" he demanded.

"I'm—"

"Don't apologize!" he snapped back. "You might regret what we did because you feel you must be loyal to a dead man, but I do not. I don't regret making love to you. I don't regret making you mine. I don't regret making you scream in pleasure as I took you in my clinic over and over again."

Susannah flushed bright red and she hoped none of the Benningtons had overheard. She cleared her throat. "Hugh, you know what we have between us cannot be. I am a widow."

"Widows get remarried. You're not a nun."

"You deserve a young, never married girl. A pure girl who doesn't have all this baggage and sorrows, as I do." Her voice turned soft. "Perhaps you don't see it now, but you will."

"I want *you.*"

Susannah didn't say anything. Even with his arrogant tone, she could see through his pain. She had broken his heart like the cruel woman she was and Susannah was too embarrassed to apologize. Instead, she looked at her feet, wishing the ground would swallow her whole.

"I think it's time for me to leave," she announced softly. "I've overstayed my welcome. Perhaps I should have never come in the first place, even though I did enjoy meeting your family."

Hugh's nostrils flared in annoyance. "No."

She frowned. "I'm all better, Hugh. You can't keep me here just because you feel like it."

He took a step towards her until her back was pressed against the wall. "You're not going back. Not until I'm sure a strong wind won't knock you down. Besides, a ruined farm is no place for a woman."

She narrowed her eyes at him. If she wasn't one hundred percent sure that Hugh would spank her for it, she would have slapped him. "Well, thankfully, I didn't ask for your opinion. It is my farm and I think it's beautiful. If you're not going to take me back, then I will just find my way home."

Hugh smiled cruelly at her as he caged her in with his arms. "With what money? You don't have any to purchase a train ticket nor a horse to take you. You've certainly made it quite clear you don't need me, Sue. Guess you're going to have to stay here with me forever."

Her green eyes widened. "This was a trap. You never had

any intention of taking me back, did you? You wanted me to rot in Larkspur Valley forever!"

He gave a little shrug and she wanted to kill him for being so smug. How could she have been so dumb as to believe he had the best intentions at heart? Hugh always did what Hugh wanted.

"You bastard!" she screamed as she attempted to slap him, but she was too slow.

Hugh gripped her wrist as he stared at her with a mocking expression. "Careful. You wouldn't want my family to hear you getting spanked, would you?"

Before she could curse him out, Lucy peeked out nervously. "Is everything all right?"

Susannah managed to break her wrist out of his grip. Her cheeks burned with anger, but she didn't want to throw a tantrum in front of everyone. "Ask him," she snarled as she went upstairs.

Susannah didn't come out for the rest of the night, which she supposed was what Hugh wanted all along.

# Chapter 11

HUGH WAS NEVER GOING to forgive her for this.

Susannah squeezed her eyes shut as the horse galloped under her towards her real home. Her farm. The horse was blissfully unaware that she was not his owner and that, in fact, she had stolen him from Steve Bennington. A sheriff who could easily have her arrested.

It hadn't been easy, that was for sure, but the argument she'd had with Hugh made it clear he wasn't going to allow her to leave. Ever.

She had left the Benningtons' second home while Lily and Iris were still sleeping, to walk into Larkspur Valley. The trip had taken a while by foot and her feet were sore by the time she made it into town, but she kept on moving.

Susannah was too much of a coward to steal Hugh's horse. He would surely spank her if he found her rummaging around when it wasn't even dawn. Not to mention, he was a light sleeper.

Anthony was too sweet and she didn't want God's condemnation if she stole his horse, so that left her with Steve. Thankfully, Steve's small barn where he kept his horses was a few feet away from the main house, so it would be next to impossible for him to overhear her.

Susannah knew taking the train was faster, but she didn't have any money nor had she ever taken a train. She left Larkspur Valley a little after five in the morning when half of the town was still sleeping.

Something Hugh didn't know about her was that she had a good memory and was an expert at reading maps. In fact, she had been the one to guide Harry to Wyoming in the first place, since his sense of direction wasn't all that good to begin with. She was fairly confident she would be able to get to the farm in one piece.

After she solved her financial situation, she would send a letter to Steve, apologizing for stealing his horse and offering payment. Susannah wasn't sure how much horses cost, but she hoped it wasn't a lot.

She fiddled with her wedding ring on her finger. She had done the right thing, hadn't she?

Hugh didn't have the authority to take her away from the farm forever. It wasn't like he was her husband. Then why did she feel so guilty for leaving him and his family behind? Why was she wondering if Hugh would come search for her? Why did being alone terrify her after she'd been alone for two years since Harry died?

Susannah didn't sleep for more than an hour on her way to the farm. She was too worried about the horse being stolen. They only rested because she and Steve's horse needed to eat and because it wasn't like Christopher's or Hugh's. It wasn't used to the long journey.

Her body sagged with relief when she finally saw her little cabin. She felt the tears pool in her eyes. She was finally home.

After putting Steve's horse in the barn and giving him

some of the food she had also stolen from him, she went inside her cabin.

A gasp escaped her lips when she looked inside.

There were dishes scattered over the entrance, rotten food stomped all over her floors, the furniture had been flipped, and it seemed like every drawer and cabinet had been pulled open and rummaged.

Burglars.

No doubt they had come across her cabin during her month-long stay with the Benningtons. They had clearly been looking for money or something of value. They must have been disappointed. She had sold everything remotely worth anything years ago.

She shook her head, forcing herself not to cry. Crying wouldn't do anything but help waste more time. Susannah pushed up her sleeves and started to work. The broken dishes were put in the trash can while the leftover food and trash were taken outside. She needed to burn them, as leaving it outside, especially the food, would just attract wild, hungry animals since it had just become spring,

Thankfully, she had a few matches left. She placed the trash into a neat pile outside as Harry had told her to do and lit a match. Susannah had to be careful; she knew how easily fires could spread. But she had done this dozens of times.

The redhead would focus on rearranging the furniture before putting it out.

While the trash burned outside, she tried her best to rearrange the furniture, but it was heavy. When she finally did, she settled down with a tired but triumphant smile on her face.

Her back and legs ached, but she wasn't sure if it was because she'd been riding for days or because the furniture was so heavy. She tiredly removed her wedding ring and placed it next to her.

She'd gained weight during her time at the Benningtons and the ring had become too tight around her wedding ring finger. Susannah would have to take it to a jeweler so they could make the band wider.

Her eyes felt heavy, reminding her she hadn't slept in days. With closed eyes, she silently told herself she would only rest her eyes for a few minutes.

---

"Susannah!"

Susannah opened her eyes when she heard the strong, masculine voice call out her name. She twisted her neck to look around and felt her heart stop inside her chest.

Fire. There was fire and smoke everywhere. How could she not have felt it? Or smell it? Had she been exhausted?

The fire was crawling up the walls and towards the roof. She was darn lucky a piece of wood hadn't fallen on her.

Hugh was standing before her, large and imposing, his blue eyes glaring at her as if he wanted to throttle her, and she couldn't blame him.

Susannah had been very stupid, indeed, to fall asleep instead of tending to the fire which was burning the trash outside like she was supposed to.

Her green eyes settled on the slight burnt marks on his forearms from when he had entered the house. Hugh probably had to push or kick the door so he could even get in to prevent Susannah from being engulfed in the flames.

Tears pooled at her eyes when she saw the redness and the skin peeling off. Hugh was hurt because of her. How could she be so selfish?

"Your arms," she whimpered. "You're hurt. Oh, Hugh, I am so sorry."

"Get up!" he said, ignoring her apology as he wrapped

his arm around her waist and dragged her out of the burning house.

Once they were outside, Susannah watched in horror as her former home collapsed under the flames. If Hugh hadn't been there, or if they had waited a second longer, they would have collapsed under the flames.

Out of the corner of her eye, she saw two of her neighbors coming with wagons filled with buckets and tubs of water from the nearby river or their own private wells.

Susannah heard someone say they had sent someone into the city to inform the fire department, but it was still a forty-minute trip, even by horse.

"Stay here!" Hugh snarled.

The redhead watched pathetically as Hugh helped her two neighbors anxiously dump the water on top of the open flames in order to prevent the fire from spreading. The fire department arrived an hour and a half later. By that time, most of the fire had been put out, and they finished the job.

One of them questioned Susannah, who meekly told them what happened. The firefighter scolded her before asking her if she had somewhere she could stay.

At that point, Hugh had placed a hand on her shoulder and told them she was staying with him.

Susannah felt numb as she watched the remains of her cabin once everyone, with the exception of Hugh, who stood quietly before her, even though his arms must surely be hurting him, had left.

Everything had either been destroyed by the fire or charred black. Before the fire, everything had been worn out so there was nothing worth saving.

Tears pooled in her eyes, but she refused to let them fall. This was her fault. She didn't deserve to cry, especially after Hugh had risked everything to save her.

"When did you know I was gone?" she asked quietly.

Hugh snorted. "After I heard Steve scream bloody murder about his horse. I put two and two together. You are a fast rider and you memorize routes fast. I will acknowledge that."

She laughed, but it was without humor. "All my stuff is gone."

"I'll buy you new stuff."

"My wedding ring is gone too. I took it off before I fell asleep."

"Perhaps it's for the best. Maybe it's God's way of saying you should move on from this place," Hugh offered gruffly as he squeezed her shoulder. For once, she didn't scold him over the lack on sensibility of his words. Maybe he did have a point. "Let's go home."

*Home.*

The word had never sounded sweeter.

## Chapter 12

"IT COULD HAVE BEEN WORSE," Ruby pointed out as she took a bite of a cookie Susannah had made for Hugh. Susannah had many leftovers because Hugh didn't particularly like sweets. "At least both of you are still alive."

Lucy bounced Lloyd on her knee. "I am still surprised the fire managed to spread so fast."

Poppy cradled her large, pregnant belly. "Both of you are just lucky you didn't inhale any of the fumes and that it wasn't summer. A little fire can cause a whole lot of damage."

Silver stuffed three cookies in her mouth while Ruby scolded her.

Iris and Lily were still at school and the four women were enjoying the beautiful March sun. All except Susannah, who still felt like the guilt was eating her alive, even though everyone kept insisting it was just a terrible accident and they should be grateful no one was hurt.

After Susannah and Hugh had double checked that there was nothing they could recover from the burnt cabin, they'd taken the horses into Laramie, where they stayed the night so both of them could get some rest. Hugh refused to let her get her own room at the hotel, for fear she might try to escape again, even though she protested it was scandalous because they were not married. Hugh didn't care.

Since he'd completed medical school in Laramie, Hugh knew many doctors from school who stayed in the city after graduation. One of them managed to patch him up and told him his burns were superficial and they would heal in a few weeks, but he warned there would probably be scarring.

The comment had caused Susannah to burst into tears as she promised she would take care of him all he wanted. This caused Hugh to be embarrassed and for his friend to laugh as he assured her he was perfectly well, though he probably shouldn't be carrying heavy things for a few weeks so as not to aggravate the injuries.

Once the diagnosis was complete, Hugh paid a man to take his and Steve's horses to Larkspur Valley so he and Susannah could take the train. He just wanted to go back home and forget this incident.

Susannah couldn't even enjoy her first train ride because she was riddled with guilt every time she saw his arms.

Since returning to Larkspur Valley, Susannah had become the model nurse, cooking and cleaning Hugh's bachelor home and fussing over him before Anthony took her to the Benningtons' home in the evening. She wanted to be helpful, but Hugh looked annoyed every time she fussed over him.

"What are you going to do now, Susannah?" Lucy asked gently as she rocked Lloyd to sleep.

Susannah's cheeks burned crimson with embarrassment. "I'm not sure." She had been wearing Ruby and Poppy's hand-me down dresses since all of her clothes had burned. Hugh had offered to purchase for her some readymade dresses from the dressmaker in town or some cloth from the mercantile to make some new ones. Lucy, apart from being the perfect rancher's wife, was apparently an expert with a needle and thread.

"Did you have any savings at a bank in Laramie?" Poppy pressed on as she put a reassuring hand on her shoulder.

"No." She sighed. "I only had a few dollars to my name if I'm being completely honest. Now, that's gone. Burned to the ground, along with everything else."

Tears stung at her eyelids. It felt like the only thing she had been doing since she returned to Larkspur Valley was cry. Even Hugh must have felt some pity for her because he hadn't scolded her for being so careless and nearly getting herself killed, but she knew her punishment would come soon enough.

Her bottom ached at the thought, even though she knew she deserved a whipping. Susannah had almost lost her life and nearly dragged Hugh along with her. She wouldn't have been able to face the Benningtons if she had ended up getting their brother killed.

"You could marry Hugh." Ruby's face brightened. "That will certainly solve all of your problems, and he completely adores you. You wouldn't have to work on winning him over when you already won him."

She blushed. "I can't marry him because I'm homeless. Besides, he already proposed and I rejected him. I doubt he will propose twice."

The three women's eyes bugged out almost comically.

"Hugh proposed and you said no?" Ruby squeaked. "Do you know how rare that is? The man is allergic to courting anyone properly. The fact he proposed is a miracle in itself. Why on earth did you say no?"

"This was weeks ago." Susannah groaned. She regretted bringing it up in the first place. "At the time, I was still mourning my dead husband. I never thought I would marry again."

"You said *at the time*." Poppy pounced like a snake. "Does this mean you're no longer in mourning? You have been a widow for two years, Sue."

Lucy's voice grew gentle. "I hope we don't seem insensitive, Susannah. We do want you to be happy, of course, but you've been mourning Harry a long time. Surely, he would want you to move on and be happy. You're still young. I doubt he would want you to be sad for the rest of your life."

Susannah's shoulders slumped. "I've made peace with Harry's death. He's never coming back. I understand that." Her eyes watered. "But all he wanted, his final wish, was that I would keep the farm running. Now, it's burnt to the ground. I feel like I failed him."

Lucy hugged her tightly while Lloyd squirmed between them. "Oh, honey, I'm sure Harry knows up in heaven that it was an accident."

"And this is your chance to stop clinging to the past." Ruby started braiding Silver's golden hair. "It isn't healthy."

Lucy glared at her, giving her a *that's not very helpful* look.

"I'm scared," Susannah whispered. "Harry and I started courting when I was fourteen. I got married at eighteen. I've never done much without anyone guiding me. What if I fail completely?"

"You've done plenty," Poppy argued. "You survived seven years living in a completely different state, without any family or friends nearby, and you kept the farm running to the best of your abilities for two years. You're strong, Susannah, in your own way. I hope you never forget it."

Ruby smirked. "Besides, you've got us. We will never let you fail. We already think of you as one of us."

Susannah sniffed. "You are all so sweet. I'm grateful."

She looked up at Poppy who knew her twin best. "Do you think Hugh will ever propose again?"

Poppy laughed. "I can certainly get the idea into his head. Discreetly, of course."

---

"You need to marry the girl," Christopher ordered sternly as the four brothers stood outside Steve's home. Ruby and Silver were already asleep and the brothers decided to meet there because Hugh was tired of being at home.

As much as he appreciated Susannah's concern over him, her fussing was driving him crazy. The only reason she wasn't glued to his side was because she spent the night with Iris and Lily to avoid his gossipy neighbors.

The first few days had been nice, having her undivided attention. He knew she was filled with guilt, but slowly, she started driving him crazy even though he knew her heart was in the right place. She was acting as if he were missing a limb instead of having a couple of burn injuries. The burn marks on his arms would heal eventually, but they would leave ugly scars.

"I'm serious, Hugh." Christopher scowled. "Either marry the girl or help her form her life somewhere else. She's too flighty and headstrong. This is not the first time she has dragged you into her mess."

Steve looked amused. "Maybe our little brother is a glutton for punishment."

"Marriage would provide stability for her, which Susannah desperately needs. Once you marry her, you will be able to keep an eye on her." Christopher glared at Anthony. "Right? Tell him he should marry her."

Anthony shifted uncomfortably. "I don't think we can tell Susannah and Hugh what to do, but marriage does bring stability and a partnership. I do believe everyone should have a partner to help them navigate life."

Christopher didn't look pleased with his answer. "Well? Are we going to see a new Mrs. Bennington soon?"

Hugh let out a puff of cigar smoke, which caused Anthony to wrinkle his nose in disgust. His younger brother really needed to loosen up, even Chris wasn't so uptight. His brothers waited impatiently for his answer.

"Of course, I'm going to marry her," he finally said.

Steve let out a whoop while Chris breathed a sigh of relief that he was finally getting married. Hugh had a feeling Christopher wouldn't feel truly at peace until Lily was married off.

"I thought you said you asked her once and she rejected you."

"Well, last time, I gave her a choice. This time, I am not."

Steve roared with laughter. "I wish I was in the room when you tell her that. She's not going to be happy, that's for sure."

Hugh's lip curled as he looked at his burnt forearms. The scarring was ugly, but nothing which wouldn't fade over time. Eventually, they would become pink, then white. "I don't care. I've given her choices in the past and all it has caused is for her to become foolish. Now, we are doing things my way."

Susannah came over the next morning like she always did, wearing one of Lucy's old gingham dresses which no longer fit in the bust area after she gave birth to Lloyd. She had added some fancy cuffs on the sleeves so Susannah wouldn't feel too bad at the fact she was wearing someone else's clothes.

Hugh had offered to buy her new clothes, underthings, and anything else she wanted, but she had stubbornly refused. Susannah wouldn't be able to once she became his lawfully wedded wife. If her pride still got in the way of accepting simple necessities, then he could always ask Ruby to go shopping for her, something the blonde loved to do.

"I'm sorry I'm late." She pushed a red curl away from her forehead. She was carrying a large basket which contained the breakfast she made every morning. Susannah had started walking from the Benningtons' second home even though it was quite a walk from town, instead of having Anthony pick her up. She said she enjoyed walking Iris and Lily to school. "I was helping Iris with an essay for her English class and then Lily wanted me to try to do a new hairdo for her. Time got away from me and I—"

"Sit down, Susannah. Put the food away," he ordered sternly.

Hugh was only taking patients in the afternoons for now, so he and Susannah could have a proper breakfast. Today, however, the time was going to be used more wisely—for her punishment.

Susannah raised an eyebrow but did as she was told and sat down in one of the chairs in his small dining area.

"We've had a few days to calm down and address what happened back at the farm. Now, young lady, it's time for your punishment."

Susannah's face paled. "But your arms—"

"Are perfectly well," he interrupted her, trying to hide the smirk on his face. "I will be returning back to work at my scheduled hours next week."

"So soon?"

"They are healed. There is no infection. Now, it's time to return to normal." He clicked his tongue. "Besides, I only need one arm to whip your defiant little ass."

Susannah bit her lower lip. "I don't suppose I could persuade you, could I? It was an accident, after all, if you recall."

"I know it was. An accident which could have cost you your life. That is not something I am willing to just sweep under the rug. You were not even supposed to be there. You were supposed to be *here*."

Hugh hadn't realized how stern his voice had gotten until Susannah flinched. "I'm sorry, Sue. But when I saw the cabin burning, I thought the worst. I thought you were truly dead. If I hadn't been following behind you, you would have been."

Susannah's eyes watered. "I'm sorry. I left out of anger. I thought you were being unreasonable. I never meant for any of this to happen. Truly."

"I believe you." He pushed another one of the dining room chairs forward. "Which is why we are going to get this spanking over with and relieve some of the guilt you are feeling."

It took a while, but Susannah finally nodded, even though her face was pale. She knew she deserved this punishment. Once she took it, the guilt she was feeling would go away.

"There's my good girl. Now, bend over the chair, lift up your skirts, and drop your drawers. Your ass needs to be bare for your punishment."

Susannah blushed an adorable shade of pink as she shuffled towards the chair and did as he said. Her drawers fell to the floor until they were wrapped around her ankles, then she pushed her dress up.

Bending over the chair, she presented her round, newly plump cheeks towards him. Susannah was so fair, he often felt like he was looking at a porcelain doll. She trembled slightly, draped over the chair, and he could tell she was anxious because, for once, she wasn't dripping wet between her legs.

A part of him wanted to forgo the punishment and just

take her to his bed. His cock agreed, given the way it was swelling inside his trousers in excitement to see Susannah's bare rump.

Hugh shook his head, ignoring his desires as he removed his belt and folded it in half. He needed to do this. Susannah would never take him seriously if he didn't. Not to mention the fact that he planned on being her husband soon and she needed to know there would be consequences if she misbehaved.

This wouldn't be a light spanking, like the first time they had met. This would be a thorough punishment. Hugh raised his belt in the air and swung it before it landed perfectly in the center of her round cheeks.

Susannah squealed at the impact. This was definitely worse than the first spanking he had given her. The first spanking had felt like love taps compared to the fire he was igniting on her ass currently.

The belt landed a second time, this time across the backs of her sensitive thighs. She shifted from foot to foot as she loosened her grip on the chair. Her eyes were quickly watering and she couldn't believe she was about to cry over two strokes of his belt.

Susannah hoped that when they looked at each other, he would see her watering eyes and stop spanking her. She was severely disappointed when a pair of cold eyes stared back while he still held the belt. It was clear he was not giving up anytime soon.

"Stay still, Sue. Hold the chair tightly." Hugh's voice was icy. "Unless you want me to tie you down."

Susannah's lips trembled as she shook her head. Hugh looked like he wasn't going to back down anytime soon.

"Face the wall. Grip the chair. Now." The belt was slapped down again, this time focusing on just the right cheek. Her nails gripped the arms of the chair as she tried her best not to squirm, but she had a feeling she was doing a very poor job of it. "Don't move. Take your spanking like a good girl."

Susannah tried her best to stay still for her spanking, but as the belt continued to slap down on her rear end, she struggled to stay still. Tears poured down her face, even knowing she deserved to be spanked. She was quite lucky she was even alive.

Dark red cheeks jiggled with each slap of the belt and she'd stopped caring about her modesty a long time ago. Hugh had already seen every nook and cranny of her. She had nothing to hide.

Her cheeks bounced rhythmically against the spanking weapon. Susannah didn't even want to think of the shameful exhibition she must be presenting to Hugh, but she didn't care. All she could think about was how hot her bottom was getting.

Despite her tears, Hugh didn't seem to want to stop spanking her. Susannah would promise anything if it meant Hugh would stop.

"Please." Her voice shook. "Please, I am so sorry, Hugh. I will never put my life in danger again. Please."

The belt crashed one more time against both cheeks, causing Susannah to yelp.

"We're done, Sue. Stop crying."

Susannah breathed a sigh of relief when she felt the belt drop to the floor. She stood up slowly, feeling the stretched skin cry out in pain. Her bottom felt hot and achy and she doubted she would be able to sit for a long time.

Her lower lip trembled when she looked back at her scorched rear end. There were pink and dark red belt marks all across both ass cheeks. Tiny, red and purple welts were scattered against both cheeks, which would no doubt itch and sting as they healed.

Susannah stared at Hugh with big, wet eyes as if silently blaming him for her misfortune.

Hugh opened his arms, his voice firm but warm. "Come here, Susannah."

She could push him away, yell at him, Lord knew he had earned a slap or two, but instead, she shuffled towards him like a sad little kitten. Hugh embraced her in his strong arms as he started rubbing her back.

Her sobs became more quiet as Hugh continued rubbing her back, shushing her quietly until she calmed down. "There, there, minx, it's all over."

"I'm sorry," Susannah choked. "I really am."

"I know. I'm going to put you down for nap. I think it will suit you."

She nodded as she buried her face in his chest.

"Sue, we are going to get married."

It wasn't a question.

"Yes, Hugh."

## Chapter 13

IF IT WERE UP to Hugh, he would have married Susannah the following day. Given his brother was the town pastor, he didn't have to wait too long to get married. It wasn't like he was planning on inviting anyone except his family.

Unfortunately for him, Susannah and the women in his family had told him they wanted time to plan a proper wedding. Even if it was just the family, the girls wanted Hugh and Susannah to have a nice wedding banquet at least, and Susannah wanted a pretty wedding dress, since all of her clothes had burned in the fire.

So far, Susannah had been wearing hand me downs from the other women. Even though Hugh had offered multiple times to purchase new clothes for her, she had refused, telling him it wouldn't be proper until they were married.

Hugh thought the whole thing was silly, but he didn't want to upset his wife-to-be. He had technically not given her a choice and forced her to marry him. He supposed he could be a little more lenient on what Susannah wanted for a wedding.

Besides, he would have the rest of their lives to spoil her

rotten, which he planned to do as soon as they got married the following month.

There wasn't much for Hugh to do as he waited for the wedding date to approach. His bachelor home was more than enough for the two of them. It wasn't as if they were going to have kids in the future. He'd even finally gotten around to purchasing a wedding band and a beautiful engagement ring in Laramie.

Susannah had sobbed for thirty minutes when he slipped the engagement ring on her ring finger. It still surprised him how emotional she could get.

Hugh didn't care much about the wedding if he was being honest. He just wanted to be married to Susannah.

---

"I hope you like it," Lucy said nervously as she came down the stairs of the house carrying a heavy looking white gown. "I keep feeling like something is missing. Look at it. If you want to remove or add something, let me know. I can do it quickly."

Ruby rolled her eyes as she started braiding her long, blonde hair. "I'm sure it's perfect, Lucy, you are the best seamstress we know. You should become a dressmaker."

Lucy blushed at the compliment. She loved sewing and knitting, but she didn't seem like the type to want to have the stress of a business looming behind her. Lucy preferred to stay at home being a wife and mother.

"The important thing is that Susannah likes it," she said modestly.

"I can't believe the wedding is a week away." Poppy placed a hand on her large belly. She still had a month to go, but it looked like she was about to pop at any moment. She hadn't complained about the weight of her belly and was excitedly waiting for the birth of her baby.

Susannah couldn't blame her. She wouldn't complain once if she could actually carry a baby. It had been hard seeing Poppy become bigger and bigger, almost as if the blonde were mocking her. She knew the thoughts were silly and childish. She was ashamed of them because Poppy had been her biggest supporter throughout her journey with Hugh.

It was so hard to be happy for someone else when they had everything you've always wanted for yourself. Especially when you yourself were empty handed. She hoped God would forgive her for her cruel thoughts. She was sincerely happy for Poppy. She hoped she would have a happy, healthy baby.

"Sue," Lucy said gently, "give me the baby and go try this on. You can use the library down the hall for privacy. We'll help you with the lacing when you are done."

Susannah stopped playing with Lloyd, who was giggling as he played with her bright red curls, to look at her wedding gown.

When they were looking through fabrics at the mercantile, she was surprised when Lucy had suggested white. She had told her a white gown would look lovely against her rosy complexion and would make her bright red hair stand out. Susannah had agreed against her better judgment, but now she realized Lucy was right.

The white gown was lovely, with a narrow waist and a fuller skirt with matching white ruffles at the bottom. The collar of the dress was trimmed with lace. Lucy had even been creative enough to add light blue ribbon around the opposite ends of the bodice. On the center of her bosom, was a dainty, faux pink rose which matched the color of her lips.

Lucy bit her lip nervously. "Do you like it? Oh, I knew we should have gone to a professional instead. The woman who made Poppy's wedding dress was lovely, maybe—"

Susannah interrupted her monologue to embrace her. "You did a wonderful job, Lucy. It's an absolutely beautiful dress."

Lloyd whined in his mother's arms as he was squished by the dress.

Lucy dabbed her eyes with a handkerchief. "I'm so glad you like your wedding present, Sue. I did it with lots of love."

"I can tell."

Ruby rolled her eyes. "Enough with the crying, it's not even noon yet. Susannah, can you please try on the dress? We still need to talk about the food for after the ceremony and the wedding cake."

Susannah did as she was told and put on the wedding dress. Ruby later came in to help tighten her corset and button the back of the dress.

She came out shyly in the elegant white gown as the women cooed over her. Silver clapped her hands gleefully as the little girl started running around in circles screaming, "Princess! Princess!"

"You look beautiful!" Lucy smiled. "I knew white would look incredible on you."

Poppy winked in her direction. "Hugh won't be able to take his eyes off you, that's for sure."

Susannah blushed as she looked at the white shoes Ruby and Steve had given her as a wedding present.

She was feeling too shy and emotional to express her thanks properly, but the women knew exactly what she was struggling to say.

After she removed her wedding dress, Susannah and the rest of her future in-laws spent the rest of the afternoon talking about the wedding food and the wedding cake. Iris had offered to do the cake since she had a talent for cake decorating.

Susannah and Hugh's wedding was going to be an intimate ceremony. Susannah didn't know anyone in town and Hugh wasn't exactly sociable. She didn't mind; she much preferred it that way. It would be nice to celebrate her wedding with just the Benningtons who quickly had become her own family.

Lucy invited all of the women to stay for dinner. Poppy refused, saying Finn would have her hide if she wasn't home on time with the horse and wagon instead of the pony she normally rode. Ruby wanted to take a fussy Silver home, and Susannah said she wanted to have supper ready for Iris and Lily when they came home from school.

Later that evening once Lily and Iris went to bed, Susannah found herself outside, looking at the night sky. The stars were shining brightly today, but the emptiness in her stomach never left her.

By this time next week, she would be Mrs. Hugh Bennington. She played with her engagement ring, still getting used to it being there instead of Harry's gold wedding band. Harry had been too poor to be able to afford both rings, so she'd only had the wedding band, but it had also been lost in the fire.

She looked at her engagement ring and smiled. It was a beautiful ring. Dainty and priceless like her, Hugh had concluded when he had slipped the ring on her finger after he returned from Laramie.

Hugh hadn't proposed, not traditionally. He'd just slipped the ring on her finger.

Strangely, she hadn't minded. Neither of them were the type to want big proposals.

Besides, she doubted Hugh would let her back out of a marriage.

They were in this together.

For life.

---

"I need to talk to you."

Hugh stopped trying to fix his tie to look annoyingly at his twin. He'd been trying to fix his tie for the past ten minutes, but his hands seemed to have become a fumbling mess. Hugh never thought he would be the type to get wedding jitters, but here he was, struggling to finish dressing himself and pacing around the room like an idiot. He was just grateful the church was less than ten minutes away and he didn't have to worry about being late. His brothers would never let him live it down if he got there after the bride.

When Hugh had heard the knock on the door, he thought it was Christopher whom he had chosen as his best man, since Anthony would be performing the ceremony. It turned out to be his twin, who had jumped out of the wagon looking like a pastry in a pink dress with her protruding belly.

He had glared at his brother-in-law Finn for allowing Poppy to storm in on the morning of his wedding, but the blond man had just shrugged. He'd always struggled to control the hard-headed Poppy and Finn had become softer with her since she became pregnant. Lord help him if he had a daughter, because both women would make him their willing slave.

"Does it have to be now?" He looked at his pocket watch. "I am getting married in less than twenty minutes and I still need to finish getting dressed. I can't keep Susannah waiting."

Poppy rolled her eyes as she started fixing his tie. "Stop being such a worrywart. I will be done in two shakes of a lamb's tail. There." She smiled. "You look very handsome."

"Poppy!" he growled. "What are you doing here?"

"Do you love her?" Poppy blurted out.

"What nonsense are you asking?"

"It's not nonsense. It's just a question. Answer it. Do. You. Love. Her?" Poppy stared at him with her sharp blue eyes, demanding an answer.

"Yes, I love her," Hugh growled back. "I wouldn't be marrying Susannah if I didn't, would I? Honestly, Pop, I don't know what goes through your head sometimes."

Poppy smiled. "I just had to make sure you were marrying for the right reasons and not because you had to get married because everyone else is." She kissed his cheek. "You look very handsome, brother. Susannah is lucky to have you."

"I'm the lucky one," he managed to say. Hugh raised an eyebrow. "And when have I ever done something because others are doing it?"

Poppy laughed.

"Pop?"

"Yes, Hugh?"

"How is she doing?" Hugh forced himself to ask the question even though he wasn't sure he really wanted the answer. "She's not regretting getting married again, right? I suppose I could have been nicer when I asked her."

Poppy shook her head sympathetically. "Then you wouldn't be you, and might I remind you that you didn't exactly ask her. Susannah is excited about the wedding. She looks beautiful; you won't be able to recognize her once Ruby, Lucy, and Lily are done with her."

"She's always been beautiful."

Poppy rolled her eyes playfully. "I never knew you were a romantic, Hugh. Susannah is quite lucky to see this side of you."

"I haven't told her," Hugh admitted softly.

"Haven't told her what?"

"That I love her." Hugh shrugged. "I've been meaning to, but I just seem to struggle to get the words out properly."

Poppy smiled so brightly, Hugh regretted saying the words in the first place. If she told their brothers, they would tease him mercilessly. "Has she?"

"No, but she has been clingier than usual, which I surprisingly don't mind."

"Well, your courting stage has been anything but traditional. She's probably feeling shy as well. Both of you need to take the plunge. You, especially, since you're the groom and you forced the whole thing. It would be nice to give her some reassurance."

"Poppy Weston, we are going to be late!"

Poppy rolled her eyes as she patted her hair, making sure it wasn't out of place. "I mean it, Hugh, don't ruin the best thing that has ever happened to you. I'll see you at the wedding."

After Poppy and Finn left, Hugh straightened up and made sure everything was where it should be. He was suddenly glad he had given the wedding rings to Christopher. For the first time in his life, he felt anxious and out of place.

In an hour, he would be a married man, after running away from commitment for so long.

Hugh took his buggy to the church. He could have walked, but he and his new bride would be going to Lucy and Christopher's for the wedding lunch and he didn't want her dress to get dirty.

"You're late," Christopher scolded, always a stickler for punctuality.

"Do you have the wedding bands?" he demanded, ignoring the question.

Christopher nodded as he pulled out a green velvet box before handing it to Lucy, who was holding Lloyd. Lloyd was the ring bearer and he was wearing a tiny, blue velvet suit his mother had made for him. Apparently, he hated it because he was mid-tantrum while wearing the uncomfortable clothes.

Poppy and Finn sat on the groom's side, giggling to each other, no doubt discussing how excited they were about their baby.

Hugh looked satisfied as he looked at the church to make sure nothing else was missing. Anthony, Lily, and Iris had decorated the church with big, fat white bows on the church's pews and there were spring flowers everywhere.

He saw Iris and Lily, the bridesmaids, wearing matching green gowns, at the back of the church as they squabbled over something. Ruby was explaining to Silver, their flower girl, what she needed to do. The toddler had a look of concentration on her precious face.

Someone placed a hand on his shoulder and Hugh actually flinched. When he turned around, he saw his brother, Anthony, dressed in his Sunday best. "Are you okay? You seem jittery."

"I'm fine," Hugh responded curtly. "Is the wedding going to start soon?"

"In about five minutes," Anthony answered patiently. "It's all right if you are a bit nervous. It is completely normal."

"I am not nervous," he insisted.

Anthony shrugged.

Five minutes later, he and Christopher were standing next to each other at the front of the church. "Smile, for God's sake," Chris grumbled. "You're acting as if you're going to be executed."

"You weren't all smiles when you married Lucy," he snapped.

"Well, that was different. I barely knew Lucy back then. You've been pining after Susannah since you met her."

Before Hugh could say anything else, the organ music started playing, letting them know the wedding was going to start soon. He took in a deep breath as he waited for his wife. He'd been waiting for this day since he met Susannah. He couldn't believe it was actually here.

The first person who came down the aisle was Lucy, holding Lloyd, who had finally gotten over his tantrum and was now chewing on the velvet ring box. Silver followed as she jumped up and down in her little green dress while she threw daisies everywhere. Iris and Lily managed to hinder their squabbling to walk down the aisle demurely as they held their bouquets made of white daisies.

Then came the bride.

Hugh was convinced he had never seen a more beautiful bride. The white gown made Susannah's bright red hair stand out, while the faux rose on her dress brought out her natural pinkness. The long, white veil had been stitched by Susannah and Lucy and covered with handmade stitches of tiny daisies, her favorite flowers.

Unlike Hugh, she didn't seem nervous, but confident. There was a brilliant smile on her face as she walked towards him while holding Steve by the arm.

Once they reached Hugh, Steve kissed her cheek and murmured something in her ear which made her giggle before he rejoined his wife.

Hugh squeezed her hand. "You look beautiful, Sue."

Susannah blushed. "And you look very handsome, Dr. Bennington."

Anthony cleared his throat as he cracked open the Bible. "Dearly beloved, we are gathered here today to join in holy matrimony Hugh Eric Bennington and Susannah Jane Cassidy."

The ceremony went much faster than expected, perhaps it was because Hugh spent all his time staring at his bride instead of paying attention, much to Anthony's annoyance.

"I declare you husband and wife. You may now kiss your bride."

Hugh lifted her veil gently to look at her pretty face. Before he could even try to kiss her, Susannah practically jumped into his arms as she kissed him first, silently letting him know she wanted him as much as he wanted her.

His family burst into loud claps as he held his hands around her waist.

"Is there any way I can convince you to skip the wedding lunch and come home with me instead?" he whispered, already knowing her answer.

"Not a chance."

He shrugged. "It was worth a shot."

After the ceremony, Hugh was forced to endure the wedding lunch and cake his sisters and sisters-in-law prepared as well as the little gifts they had purchased for the happy couple.

Hugh knew he was being ungrateful, but as much as he loved his family, he wanted to spend some alone time with his wife.

"What should we do next?" Poppy asked four hours later as she snuggled next to her husband.

Hugh jumped out of his chair, gripping Susannah's hand tightly. "We are going home!"

Steve clicked his tongue. "You could be a little more discreet."

Ruby giggled.

Susannah blushed while she pinched her new husband on the cheek, silently scolding him for embarrassing her even though he could see how tired she was. It had been a long day for everyone.

After Susannah and Hugh said their goodbyes and took

the leftover wedding cake home, they found themselves back in Hugh's buggy on the way back into town.

"I've never lived in the center of town before," she mused as they approached her new home which was attached to the practice. "Even when I was living with my family back in Kansas, we lived on a farm. How is it?"

"Less exciting than living in a city, but more interesting than living in the countryside. Though I must warn you, the people can be gossipy," he warned as he stopped the buggy.

She shrugged. "I can manage. It will be nice to have Ruby and Anthony close by and I'll still be able to say hello to Lily and Iris when they go to school. Besides, if I keep to myself, no one will have anything negative to say."

Hugh doubted it would be true, but he didn't want to break her hopes. He scooped her up in his arms.

She burst into loud, adorable giggles as she wrapped her arms around his neck. "Hugh! What are you doing? Put me down!"

Hugh grinned at her. "I am just carrying my bride home. I believe tradition dictates it."

Susannah snuggled against his neck as he took in the scent of sweet vanilla soap and the daisies from earlier.

Somehow, he managed to open the door and take her upstairs to their bedroom without dropping her.

Susannah's eyes widened when he took her into the bedroom. It was the first time she had seen it.

His room was terribly plain, with only the necessary furniture. Susannah looked like she was struggling for something nice to say about it which caused him to laugh as he helped her stand up. "I know it's plain, but you can decorate however you want. Nothing too frilly, I don't want to feel like I'm living inside one of those ruffled throw pillows women love so much," he warned.

"A little color might be nice, so it doesn't look so sad," was all she said.

"I have accounts in all the stores, just have them put everything under my account and I'll pay them later. You have to get all new stuff for yourself as well since you lost everything."

Susannah bit her lower lip. Hugh could practically hear her thoughts. Susannah was used to being poor, as Harry had never had money in his pockets. "I don't want to be a burden to you when we just got married."

He tweaked her nose. "You are not a burden. I knew having a wife was going to come with expenses. I am serious, Sue, once things settle down, you need to go shopping, or else." He squeezed her rump. "Money is not an issue and unless you are buying a fur coat, I can afford it. Believe me, you don't want me picking out your clothes. I hope you are a fan of green and yellow stripes."

She choked on a laugh. "No, Hugh, those two colors would look terrible together."

He kissed her. "Then pick your own clothes. You behaving like a martyr during the entirety of our marriage is not ideal."

Susannah nodded shyly as she tugged on his suit jacket. "Speaking of clothes, Dr. Bennington, I think it's time we take yours off."

He roared with laughter. "Are you trying to seduce me, Mrs. Bennington?"

The redhead bit her lip nervously. "Is it working?"

Hugh started to remove her frilly wedding dress. He wanted to make sure he didn't loosen any buttons or rip it like last time; otherwise, his new wife would have a fit. "Very much so, Mrs. Bennington."

Susannah blushed. "I like it when you call me that."

"I like saying it," he murmured as he kissed her.

Their wedding clothes fell to the floor until both of them were gloriously naked. He kissed every inch of her body, enjoying the pleased shudders of his wife as her eyes shone with her desire.

It was the first time they had made love without it feeling like a dirty, little secret and he was determined to enjoy every second of it.

Hugh's teeth scraped against her sensitive, peach-colored nipples as little squeals of pleasure escaped from her lips. "Do you like this?" he murmured as he squeezed one breast.

"Yes." Susannah trembled. "I love how you squeeze them."

Hugh smirked as he gently bit her neck, leaving behind teeth marks. "I love you, Sue."

Susannah blinked back in wonder. "You love me?"

"Yes." His lips trailed from her forehead down to her chin. "I've been wanting to tell you for weeks."

"Then, why haven't you?"

"I've been a coward."

"The mighty Hugh Bennington was afraid of rejection?" Susannah sobered. "Then again, I haven't been particularly kind to you, either, clinging to my dead husband."

Susannah cocked her head to the side before pressing a hand against his cheek. "I love you too, Hugh. So much. I'm sorry, I should have told you this before. I guess I was scared too." She smiled teasingly. "I've loved you since I saw you holding my drawers that January evening."

Hugh laughed as he scooped her up in his arms and she wrapped her thighs around his waist. "You brat!" He pressed her back against the wall.

Hugh squeezed her buttocks as he plunged his erect cock into her. Susannah's back slammed against the wall. Her small breasts jiggled against each stroke as he enjoyed watching them bounce against each other.

He liked being inside Susannah, even more so now that she was officially his wife, and especially since they had fought so much to get into this point of their lives.

Susannah felt incredibly tight as her wet quim milked him tightly. He felt like he was going to explode inside her before Susannah managed to reach her pleasure, which was simply unacceptable to him.

His new wife bounced on his manhood as her nails dug against his skin, leaving behind pink, half-moon shaped marks. She was close; he could see it by the way she was closing her eyes tightly.

Squeezing her rump tightly in his hands, he pushed her forward so her clit was rubbing against his lower stomach with each stroke. He enjoyed feeling her hot, wet pussy rubbing against him.

Susannah screamed in his ear as she orgasmed, before she limply held on to him as his seed dripped down her thighs.

Hugh made sure she didn't fall.

Hours later, after the both of them were exhausted from making love, they cuddled next to each other in Hugh's bed. Hugh had his arm around Susannah while she snuggled against his chest like a content kitten.

Hugh was drifting off to sleep when he heard Susannah's trembling, vulnerable voice. "Hugh, promise me one thing."

"What is it?"

"Promise me that you won't die." Susanna's voice shook. "I can't lose another man I love. I don't ever want to be a widow again. If someone is going to die first in this relationship, it is going to be me."

Hugh raised an eyebrow. "And don't you think I would miss my wife? I'm never planning on remarrying, Sue."

Susannah bit her lip. "It seems we are both the losing party."

"This is a depressing topic for our wedding night." Hugh held her close, "The truth of the matter is we don't know what will happen in the future. The only thing we can do is enjoy every moment we can."

She nodded. "I hope we can be together forever. Even after death."

"Oh, we will, Sue. I'll make sure of it," he told her solemnly.

# Chapter 14

POPPY GAVE birth in early May, to a healthy, nine-pound baby boy who everyone said looked like an angel come to life. Finn and Poppy decided to name the baby Paul Weston, after Poppy's beloved father. The labor had been hard and long, but Poppy said it had been worth every painful contraction to see her beloved son whom she had waited so long for.

When she started having birthing pains, Susannah offered to help Hugh, even if the only thing she knew about childbearing was what she had seen in animals. Hugh told her childbirth could get long and complicated and that it might be better if she kept Finn company instead.

At the time, Susannah thought it was a snub, but later, she decided it was the smartest thing he could have assigned her to do.

Finn had been a nervous mess and grew more nervous, the longer Poppy cried out in pain. At one point, Susannah had to take him outside to get him away from his wife's cries. He kept going inside her room to try and soothe her until Hugh kicked him out.

Twice, he had vomited from the anxiety of waiting to see

if his wife and baby were all right. Susannah even had to hold him up when Hugh told him that Poppy was fine, just extremely tired, and that she'd given birth to a healthy baby boy.

"He's beautiful, Pop!" Lucy cooed the next day, once she, Ruby, Lily, and Iris had come to see the baby. Poppy grinned like a proud mother.

Ruby cocked her head to the side. "He's a big boy too. No wonder you were screaming for hours. When I gave birth to Silver, I felt like I was being split open and she was small. Peeing must hurt like hell!"

"Ruby!" Iris scolded. Lily's eyes widened in horror.

"He was worth it." Poppy looked lovingly at her son who was curled up against her breast. He had honey-colored curls and bright pink cheeks. She and Finn had been over the moon since the birth and spent all their time fussing over baby Paul.

"He looks just like both of you." Susannah smiled. Both Poppy and Finn were fair-haired, but Paul had the same shade as his mother and the Bennington blue eyes.

"Thankfully, he doesn't have my temper," Poppy sighed tiredly. "He only cries when he's hungry. He's such a good baby."

Iris snorted. "He should be, after thirty-six hours of labor."

Lily shifted from foot to foot. "Oh, can I hold him, please Pop? I washed my hands."

Poppy nodded as she placed her son in Lily's arms. Poppy had raised Lily since she was a baby, when their mother died in childbirth. It was like she was watching her grown baby hold her newborn. "Be careful with his head, Lil. He likes to squirm around."

Lily nodded as she looked at the tiny baby. "Oh, Poppy, he's so sweet. I'm glad you named him after

Daddy. You're so lucky, it's like having your very own doll."

Ruby bumped her on the shoulder. "You're next, Lily."

Iris scowled. "Don't encourage her. She needs to finish school first, and there is no way Christopher will allow her to court yet."

Ruby laughed. "I was joking. Besides, you should probably get married before Lily. You are the oldest after all."

Iris flushed. "I'm never going to get married, you know that. I'm prepared to be a spinster for the rest of my life if it means I can teach." Iris had recently graduated from school, and much to her brothers' misfortune, she was still hell bent on being a teacher.

Ruby rolled her eyes. "I still don't understand why you want to teach for the rest of your life. I said the same thing about marriage and babies before your brother forced me to be his lawfully wedded wife."

"I don't hear you complaining now," Iris grumbled.

Ruby smirked. "He makes it up to me in other ways." She rubbed her flat stomach.

Lucy was the first one to catch on. "Ruby! Are you pregnant?"

Pinkness bloomed around the blonde's face. "I'm two months along. The baby should be born in December of this year. Silver is going to have a sibling and Lloyd and Paul are going to have a little cousin to play with."

Ruby was surrounded by cheers of congratulations while Susannah felt her own smile falter. She was happy for Ruby, she truly was, because she knew how much Ruby adored her daughter and husband. But it felt like she was surrounded by babies and pregnant women.

Back on the farm, she had been busy and alone, so even though she was aware of her infertility, it was always at the back of her mind. Since coming to Larkspur Valley,

Susannah felt constantly silently mocked for her infertility, though she knew it wasn't done on purpose.

In spite of the fact she was now married to Hugh and in full domestic bliss, her longing for a child had never disappeared. In fact, it seemed to have grown stronger even since she'd remarried.

She would give anything to be able to carry Hugh's child —to have a little boy or girl who had the famous Bennington blue eyes and to grow round with child.

But the fact of the matter was she would never get pregnant. Her house would never be filled with little ones, and if Hugh died before she did, she would once again be alone.

Susannah, of course, adored her new niece and nephews, but her heart still longed for her own child.

"I'll make us some tea," she declared and was proud that her voice didn't shake.

Lucy squeezed her arm in sympathy.

Susannah hadn't told any of the women about her infertility, but she suspected Hugh had, in order to avoid anyone asking about when they were going to expand their family. She was just glad the women hadn't said anything. She didn't want their pity even if their hearts were in the right place.

After she put the tea kettle on the stove, Susannah went to get some fresh air. She needed to get away from all the baby news.

As soon as she was safely outside, she felt the tears fall down her cheeks while her body shook because of how strongly she was crying.

Why couldn't she have a baby? It wasn't fair! Why couldn't God bless her with even one child? She had been a good wife to Harry and she planned to be a good wife to Hugh, so why wouldn't God bless her with her own little one?

Susannah was tired of waiting, of hoping, of crying in

despair every time she got her monthly. She felt like she was being left starving in a cage while everyone else went to experience motherhood.

Her mother often told her life wasn't fair, but she'd never expected it to be so darn cruel.

Susannah felt someone wrap their arms around her shoulders and she gasped. She hoped it wasn't Finn. She wouldn't be able to take his pity and she didn't want to make him feel bad so soon after his son's birth.

Instead, she recognized her husband's scent as he pulled her into a hug. "Susannah, what on earth is wrong? Why are you crying? Is it the baby? Poppy? Talk to me, I can't understand you with all of your crying."

"Poppy's baby is beautiful." Hugh looked confused. "And Ruby told us she's pregnant again."

"Well, the second piece of news isn't strange. She and Steve are always attached at the hip. I'm surprised she didn't get pregnant again sooner." His voice had grown gentle as he pushed back a piece of red hair. "It doesn't explain why you've been crying, though."

"I'm jealous," she confessed. "Horribly envious. I know it makes me sound like a terrible person and perhaps I am, but, Hugh, I want a baby. A baby to call my own. I am so happy for your sister and Ruby, but this day just serves to remind me of what I can't have. What I will never have." She shook her head. "Ignore me. I'm being silly and terribly selfish."

Hugh shook his head. "No, you're not. Your feelings are perfectly valid. It's to be expected; you've been waiting to be a mother for so long."

Susannah was glad she wasn't met with pity. Her new husband was a practical person.

He touched her hip. "Let me check on Poppy and Paul, and then we will go home and pack a bag."

"Why?"

"You'll see."

They took the train to Laramie, and once or twice, she asked him where they were going exactly, but Hugh wouldn't give her an answer. Instead, she was left to shift uncomfortably while she thought of a reason why they would head into the city.

She couldn't think of any.

When they arrived in Laramie, they took refuge in a hotel which was close to Hugh's former medical school. Still, her husband didn't give her any clue of why they were there. Instead, he told her it was a surprise.

They went to dinner at a nice restaurant, and although Susannah appreciated the sweet gestures from her usual, non-romantic husband, she couldn't help but be suspicious. However, she also knew her husband wasn't the type to reveal something he didn't want to.

The next morning, they dressed quickly and ate a small breakfast at the hotel. Hugh then ordered a carriage to take them to 62nd Street.

"Where are we going?" she finally asked him quietly as the carriage rode on.

There was a trace of a smile on his face. "You'll see."

The carriage stopped in front of a large, gray building which looked like a school. There was a plaque which read, *Francis Scott Orphanage*.

She stared at him with wide, green eyes as if she couldn't believe what was happening. "Why are we at an orphanage?"

"Because there isn't any in Larkspur Valley," he said as if it should have been obvious as he helped her out of the carriage. "I know you can't carry a child, Sue, but it doesn't mean you can't have a family. Family is not just blood, you know."

Susannah's eyes were wet with tears and she feared she

would start crying at any moment. "Do you want a family? We never spoke of it."

Hugh shrugged. "You're my family. I never thought of children if I'm being honest. I would be happy all the same if it was just us until death do us part. But you want children, my love. I don't want to see your heart breaking anymore. So, I thought this would be a fair compromise. If you want a child, then I want a child. We will do our best to raise him or her, so they don't become an obnoxious prick."

"Does your family know? What do they think?"

"Only Poppy knows, because we had to talk about something while we waited for Paul to make his arrival. She won't say anything because she knows we want to make the announcement. Don't worry, my family want us to be happy. They will accept any child we adopt as our own."

Susannah wrapped her arms around her husband and hugged him tightly, to the surprise of onlookers around them. "Thank you," she whispered. "Thank you so much, Hugh. You have no idea how much I appreciate this."

Hugh looked slightly embarrassed by all the public displays of affection, but he managed to kiss her forehead. "Let's go inside. Mrs. Mitchum is expecting us."

"Mrs. Mitchum?"

"She's the lady who runs the orphanage. I've been corresponding with her for a few weeks." He pressed his hand on the small of her back. "She doesn't have babies we can adopt, but there are plenty of young children we can take home with us."

"I don't care about the age range," she admitted. "I just want to be a mother, but I suppose a small child would be lovely. Seeing Silver and Lloyd play around makes me want to be surrounded by children."

He grimaced. "Then you haven't spent enough time with them. They can be little devils when they want to be."

Mrs. Mitchum turned out to be a thin, tall woman, with a rather large nose, wearing a gray dress. She was polite, but cold, as she addressed them. She ran the orphanage with strict rules and decorum, but seemed to treat the children well even though she lacked affection.

"This is the nursery," Mrs. Mitchum announced as she opened the door. "This is where we keep children under the age of six who are not old enough to go to school."

The room was filled with about fifteen little boys and girls of various ages. A middle-aged woman watched them while she needlepointed. The children were wearing clean clothes, but with obvious patches and worn out. She made a mental note to ask her husband if they could donate money before they left.

Susannah's heart ached. She wanted to adopt all of them, but she knew her husband would have a coronary if she suggested it.

The children were playing with toys, oblivious to the adults in the room.

Mrs. Mitchum cleared her throat. "Well, take a look around. See what you like." She made it sound as if Susannah was purchasing a new hat. "I will be in my office when you have reached your decision."

Susannah looked at Hugh, but for once, her husband looked uncomfortable. It seemed the idea of impending fatherhood had finally reached him. "Well, go on, Sue. I will be happy with whatever decision you make."

She took his hand gently in hers as she guided him around the room, until they reached a little boy.

He couldn't be more than four or five years old, with dirty blond hair. What caught her attention was that his eyes were the same shade of blue as the Bennington siblings.

The little boy was playing with a small toy car and he

seemed confused when Hugh and Susannah interrupted him.

"Hello," Susannah introduced herself softly, "my name is Susannah Bennington."

"That's a long name."

Susannah giggled. "Well, my husband calls me Sue." She squeezed Hugh's hand. "This is my husband, Hugh."

Hugh awkwardly ruffled the boy's hair which he did not seem to appreciate. "What's your name?"

"Isaac," the child said sweetly.

Susannah wanted to wrap him up in blankets and take him home to snuggle with him. "How old are you, Isaac?"

"Four."

Susannah smiled as she kissed his forehead. "You're such a sweet boy." She hesitated as she looked at Hugh. Hugh squeezed her shoulder. "How would you like to come home with us?"

Isaac looked perplexed and she prepared herself for a rejection. "Do you and Hugh have candy?"

Hugh laughed. "It can be arranged."

Isaac smiled.

Susannah was afraid she was going to cry tears of joy. "I think we found our boy."

---

## Epilogue

---

SIX YEARS LATER, *1879*

"Isaac!" Hugh's cheeks were flushed red with a mix of anger and worry as he struggled to chase after his ten-year-old son who was riding in front of him without a care in the world. Especially for someone who didn't have a proper saddle on.

His thighs burned as he motioned his horse to pick up the speed. His horse whinnied in protest. Hugh couldn't exactly blame him. They were both middle aged now and weren't a match for a pony and a rebellious ten-year-old.

This was one of the many times he was glad Isaac was an only child. If this one child was the cause of him sprouting gray hair early, he couldn't imagine what it was like to deal with more than one, especially since his son was a handful. Hugh shuddered as his son's teenage years weren't too far off.

Hugh hadn't exactly been a model teenager, but he was glad Isaac tended to be a jokester and a prankster, rather than aggressive like Hugh had been.

Susannah and he had talked about the possibility of adopting more children, but they had never really made it a priority after the first adoption. They both agreed Isaac was enough and they loved him to pieces. Besides, they had plenty of nieces and nephews to spoil.

Even though Susannah had just turned thirty-one and Hugh was thirty-four, neither of them seemed fond of the idea of returning to the days of babyhood. Isaac was ten and he was in school for most of the day, and he sometimes helped his Uncle Christopher and Uncle Finn, along with his cousins, with the work at the ranch after school. That left Dr. and Mrs. Bennington with plenty of alone time for each other.

As Hugh had pointed out, Isaac gave them the work and the worry of six children, but they both loved him dearly.

Hugh sometimes couldn't believe how fast time could pass. Sometimes it felt like it was just yesterday when he and his wife had brought Isaac home from the orphanage, and now here they were, raising a ten-year-old.

"Got you!"

Hugh managed to wrap an arm around Isaac's scrawny waist, lift him up from his pony, and settle him on the back of his own saddle in one quick motion. Isaac whined in protest as Hugh tied an extra rope around the pony's neck to bring him back with them.

Once the pony was settled, he turned back to glare at his son. "What did I tell you about riding without a saddle? Do you want to break your foolish neck? I told you not to keep worrying your mother."

Isaac pouted as he pressed his cheek against his father's back. "You said it was okay if I took Marshmallow out for a ride so he could stretch his legs."

"Yes, with a saddle, and a 'ride' does not mean running as if you're chasing after a criminal. Leave that to your Uncle Steve."

Isaac scowled, obviously not pleased. "Fine." He mumbled something underneath his breath.

"What was that?"

"Nothing, sir." He sulked like a spoiled brat.

"I will tan your sorry behind if you keep acting like a lunatic."

Isaac pretended he hadn't heard.

When they reached home, Isaac managed to jump from the horse before Hugh had fully stopped, earning him another scolding from his father.

His wife squealed in delight when Isaac jumped into her arms like he had when he was a child. He was growing heavy, though, and she sometimes lost her balance.

A year after they adopted Isaac, Hugh and Susannah moved away from town, ot to the country to another piece of land which belonged to the Benningtons. With the help of his brothers and his sisters' husbands along with a few men they'd hired, they managed to build a two-story house. The house had three bedrooms, a small library, and even an office for Hugh.

Susannah had grown tired of living in the loud, gossipy town and preferred somewhere quieter. As he grew older, Isaac wanted to spend more time with his cousins who mostly resided in the country and wanted more space to play. Hugh didn't mind the move, as long as it made his family happy and the journey into town wasn't terrible. He'd even used his bachelor home to expand his medical practice and he'd hired a young doctor to help him with patients, which allowed him to spend more time with his family.

"Mommy, Daddy is being mean to me." The little brat actually had the audacity to hide behind his mother's skirts while a little smile played on his lips.

"Do you want to tell your mother you were riding without a saddle, or should I?" Hugh raised an eyebrow.

"Isaac!" Susannah ran her fingers through his dark blond hair. "That's dangerous. You could fall and break your neck, and then where would we be?"

Isaac shook his head. "Daddy can fix it. He's a doctor."

Hugh sighed as he kissed his wife. "That's not how it works, son. A broken neck is not easy to fix, almost impossible. Many people who break their necks die instantly. Which is why you should always use a saddle. Do not make me tell you again."

Isaac sighed dramatically. "Okay."

Susannah kissed the top of his head. "Now, wash your hands, you two. Dinner is getting cold."

Once Isaac disappeared into the washroom, Hugh pressed his forehead against Susannah's. "How much longer until he moves into his own home?"

Susannah giggled. "Don't act like you don't enjoy fatherhood. He keeps you young."

"He gives me gray hairs."

"Isaac is Isaac. We wouldn't have him any other way, and you know it." Susannah gave him a dainty kiss. "Now, let's finish dinner quickly so we can put him to bed. I want some alone time with my husband."

Hugh smiled as he squeezed her waist. "Whatever my wife desires."

# Annabelle Marin

Annabelle Marin is a twenty-something romantic who lives in sunny California. When she isn't writing she enjoys daydreaming, watching way too much TV, and cuddling with her pets.

Her books are sweet erotic romances with domestic discipline. In her books you can expect: a spoonful of sweetness, a dash of sass, a cup of naughtiness, and an abundance of romance.

You can follow Annabelle on Facebook, Instagram, Goodreads, and Bookbub for exciting updates on upcoming books!

Facebook-https://www.facebook.com/annabelle.marin.940/
Instagram-https://www.instagram.com/
missannabellemarin/
Bookbub-//www.bookbub.com/profile/annabelle-marin
Goodreads-www.goodreads.com/author/show/21061973.
Annabelle_Marin

Don't miss these exciting titles by Annabelle Marin and Blushing Books!

*Stand Alone Titles*

Endless Paradise
Between Kisses & Lies

Letters to Holly
On the Dotted Line
His Southern Belle

*Earthly Mates Series*
The Alien's Mate

*The Benningtons Series*
Holy Matrimony
Strawberry Kiss
Pink Ribbon
Darling Minx

*The Hollis Sisters Series*
The Affair
The Scandal
The Passion

*The Stevenson Brothers Series*
The Rancher Orders a Bride
The Pastor Takes a Wife
The Sheriff Finds a Fiancée

*Vintage Beauties Series*

Bless Her Heart
Becoming a Gibson Girl
The Modern Housewife
Vintage Beauties Collection

*The Bride Series*

The Unwilling Mrs.

The Unattainable Bride
The Unexpected Wife

*Anthologies*

12 Naughty Days of Christmas 2021

# Blushing Books

Blushing Books is one of the oldest eBook publishers on the web. We've been running websites that publish spanking and BDSM related romance and erotica since 1999, and we have been selling eBooks since 2003. We hope you'll check out our hundreds of offerings at http://www.blushingbooks.com.

# Blushing Books Newsletter

Please join the Blushing Books newsletter
to receive updates & special promotional offers.
You can also join by using your mobile phone:
Just text **BLUSHING** to 22828.